Her head snaps back to me.

"Did you just come to make conversation, or are you here for a reason?"

"I'm here to propose a mutually beneficial arrangement." I smile at her, the smile I wield before I offer people what they desire. "One that would include me signing over the deed to Grey House."

Even the air seems to still as she stares at me. Then she inhales sharply and time resumes. Her lips part as her eyes move between the house and me.

"What price are you asking?"

"A reasonable and affordable one."

I reach into my pocket and pull out a black velvet box. The confusion on her face would be amusing if so much didn't hinge on her saying one specific word.

"What..."

Her voice trails off as I flip open the lid to reveal a ten-carat diamond set into a platinum band decorated with smaller but no less fine diamonds.

"Your hand in marriage."

Brides for Greek Brothers

Saying "I do" is only the start!

Lucifer Drakos was the devil incarnate. Never does that become more apparent than at the reading of his will. In order for each of his three sons to receive their billion-dollar inheritance, they must marry. And stay in wedded bliss for one whole year...

For Gavriil, Raphail and Michail, making it up the aisle is the easy part. There's no way they'll let Lucifer win. But staying wed to the three women who challenge every tenet of their lone-wolf existence? That's the hard part...

Read Gavriil's story in
Deception at the Altar
Available now!

And look out for Raphail and Michail's stories, coming soon!

DECEPTION AT THE ALTAR

EMMY GRAYSON

Harlequin
PRESENTS

If you purchased this book without a cover you should be aware that this book is stolen property. It was reported as "unsold and destroyed" to the publisher, and neither the author nor the publisher has received any payment for this "stripped book."

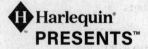

Harlequin®
PRESENTS™

ISBN-13: 978-1-335-93943-2

Deception at the Altar

Copyright © 2024 by Emmy Grayson

Recycling programs for this product may not exist in your area.

All rights reserved. No part of this book may be used or reproduced in any manner whatsoever without written permission.

Without limiting the author's and publisher's exclusive rights, any unauthorized use of this publication to train generative artificial intelligence (AI) technologies is expressly prohibited.

This is a work of fiction. Names, characters, places and incidents are either the product of the author's imagination or are used fictitiously. Any resemblance to actual persons, living or dead, businesses, companies, events or locales is entirely coincidental.

For questions and comments about the quality of this book, please contact us at CustomerService@Harlequin.com.

TM and ® are trademarks of Harlequin Enterprises ULC.

Harlequin Enterprises ULC
22 Adelaide St. West, 41st Floor
Toronto, Ontario M5H 4E3, Canada
www.Harlequin.com

Printed in Lithuania

MIX
Paper | Supporting responsible forestry
FSC® C021394

When **Emmy Grayson** came across her mother's copy of *A Rose in Winter* by Kathleen E. Woodiwiss, she snuck it into her room and promptly fell in love with romance. Over twenty years later, Harlequin Presents made her dream come true by offering her a contract for her first book. When she isn't writing, she's chasing her kids, attempting to garden or carving out a little time on her front porch with her own romance hero.

Books by Emmy Grayson

Harlequin Presents

Cinderella Hired for His Revenge
His Assistant's New York Awakening

The Van Ambrose Royals

A Cinderella for the Prince's Revenge
The Prince's Pregnant Secretary

Hot Winter Escapes

An Heir Made in Hawaii

Diamonds of the Rich and Famous

Prince's Forgotten Diamond

The Diamond Club

Stranded and Seduced

Visit the Author Profile page
at Harlequin.com.

To my mom, who helped me bring this
enemies-to-lovers to life and gave Juliette a voice.

And to four spring souls lost far too soon.
You will always be remembered.

CHAPTER ONE

Gavriil

WALKING INTO MY father's will-reading seven minutes late is satisfying. The old man, selfish as he was, was a stickler for punctuality.

I glance to my right as I walk in. The staggering sight of hundreds of skyscrapers clustered together on a tiny island never ceases to take me aback. New York City, with its gleaming steel and frantic energy, is a far cry from Malibu, where I currently live. Alessandra Wright, my father's estate lawyer, offered to fly to California or even to Greece, where my older half brother, Rafael, lives. I don't know what reason Rafe gave for declining her offer. We talk, yes. But it's usually work. Drakos Development, the largest property development firm in the world, is the glue that binds us together.

Blood certainly doesn't. That was my reason for telling Alessandra no. I've carved out a nice life for myself in Malibu. A mansion on three acres with its own beach, a private jet that can fly me from Los Angeles to anywhere in the world, and a professional reputation I earned through hard work and even harder dealings. I took the North American division of Drakos and transformed it from passable to powerhouse.

I want nothing of Lucifer Adomos Drakos anywhere near my personal paradise. Including this damned will. Family lore says my grandfather named his only child after the devil because my grandmother died giving birth to him. Whatever the reason, he more than lived up to his moniker. He was greedy and brutal. The world is a better place without him.

I turn away from the view, the towers and high-rises like jagged teeth stabbing into the sky, and focus on the two people sitting near the far window. Rafe is reviewing a thick sheaf of papers, his back ramrod straight. His black hair, combed back into submission from a broad forehead, accentuates his narrow face and sharp chin. My mouth twists into a slight grimace as I draw near. He looks more like our father every day, a point I know he wouldn't appreciate. Neither of us had any love for the man who sired us.

He glances up. Pale blue eyes meet mine. The one and only characteristic we share. It marks us. Rafe rarely displays emotion, so I have no way of knowing if it haunts him the way it does me; looking in the mirror and seeing the eyes of our father staring back.

I hate it.

"You're late."

"I am." I circle around the desk to where a tall, slender woman is standing to greet me. "Alessandra."

She smiles slightly and accepts my kiss to the cheek. The woman could have been a model, with auburn hair falling just past her shoulders and a jawline that could have been carved from marble. Instead, Alessandra Wright became

one of the youngest and most sought-after estate lawyers
in the world.

"You look stunning. If you're free this evening, we could
have dinner. Strictly business," I add with a suggestive
smile.

Alessandra rolls her eyes as she takes a seat in a straight-
backed office chair. For all our teasing and flirting over the
past few months, nothing would ever happen between us.
Not only do I not mix business with pleasure, but she's not
my type. One day, Alessandra will want—and deserve—
a husband and a family. She's got *long-term relationship*
written all over her.

"As promising as that sounds, I'll have to decline." She
glances down at her watch and frowns. "Hopefully Michail
will join us sooner rather than later."

I tap my fingers on the plush leather armrest once, twice.
Michail Drakos. Another half brother. One neither Rafe nor
I have ever met. We learned of his existence this morning
after a revised will was delivered by courier. It didn't escape my notice that our recently discovered brother bears
the moniker of a celestial being, just like Rafe and me. Lucifer had a nasty sense of humor.

I'm sure Rafe had an entire dossier put together within
an hour of receiving the will. I, on the other hand, spent
the last few hours pretending like Michail didn't exist. No
different than the last thirty-two years of my life.

My chest hardens. It hadn't surprised me that there was
another child.

But *Theós*, it hurt.

My father had called eight days before he died. The last
time we ever spoke. I almost didn't answer. I still don't
know why I accepted the call. But I answered. The raspy

weakness of his voice cut me deeper than it should have as he whispered "Hello, *yiós*."

My father was dying. He was dying and, for the first time in years, he'd called me. He'd called me *son*.

For one moment, the world stood still. I waited, letting threads of hope creep in. Hope for words of apology, of pride, of something other than the decades of scorn that had chased me.

Then time slammed back to its regular breakneck pace with his next words.

"There's someone I need to tell you about."

Thinking that Lucifer gave a damn about his bastard son was a moment of weakness. I knew better. When you care about someone, you give them power. The power to control, to manipulate.

To hurt.

Like realizing that my father's last words would have been about a son born after Rafe but before me. A son invited to today's will-reading, which means he's getting something even though he didn't survive a childhood with Lucifer criticizing his every move. Reminding him that he was less, would always be less.

I brush aside my juvenile pain. Lucifer can bequeath whatever the hell he wants to Michail. As long as it doesn't involve anything with my share of Drakos Development. I'll fight that to the highest court in any country and win.

A knock sounds on the door. My fingers tighten into a fist.

"Enter," Alessandra calls.

A man strides in, barely restrained anger radiating off his large frame. Taller than Rafe or me, with thick shoulders and a tense jaw. The only thing that confirms he's a by-product of Lucifer's numerous affairs is the eyes.

Pale blue and snapping with fury as he sweeps his gaze over Rafe, then me, then Alessandra.

His step falters. Just a moment, but I see it. My head snaps between him and Alessandra. But she doesn't bat an eye. She simply regards him with a professional expression bordering on bored. Maybe he's surprised by Alessandra's stunning looks.

Or maybe he's just a misogynistic idiot like his father.

"Mr. Drakos." She stands and offers her hand across the desk. "Thank you for joining us."

He eyes her hand like it's poisonous.

"My name is Sullivan." His voice is gravelly. "Not Drakos."

"Don't know where you're from, *adelfós*," I say casually, "but it's usually polite to shake someone's hand."

Michail's head swings around. He stares daggers at me. I give him a small smirk in return. Wit is a weapon I wield well.

A weapon and a shield.

"Who the hell are you?"

I settle deeper into my chair as my smile grows. "Your baby brother. Shall we hug, or does the occasion of our reunion warrant a familial kiss on the cheek?"

He snarls. The man actually snarls.

"Boys."

Alessandra's voice rings out, icy enough to quell even my humor. She starts to turn away. Michail's hand stabs out and grabs hers, his mammoth fingers swallowing hers in a tight grasp.

"Sorry, Miss Wright." Michail's voice comes out strangled, as if he can barely choke out the apology. "I don't want to be here."

"Then why are you here?"

Rafe finally speaks. Cold, with a thread of steel woven through his words, as usual. The man isn't known for his warm and fuzzy feelings. But the one thing he does care about? Drakos Development. If he sees Michail as a threat, God help our half brother.

Michail releases Alessandra's hand and stalks over to a window on the far side of the room, then leans casually against the glass with America's most populated city at his back.

"My reasons are my own."

Alessandra sighs as she eases into her chair.

"If you're all done seeing whose is bigger, let's proceed."

She shoots me a glance that tells me to keep the joke on the tip of my tongue to myself. I respond with a wink, which nets me another roll of her eyes and the tiniest quirk of her lips.

"Gentlemen, I will now read your father's final will and testament. Please reserve any questions for the end."

Any trace of humor disappears. I stay reclined, keep my slight smile. But inside I'm coiled tight. I know I'll survive, no matter what the will says.

But losing my life's work will be like a death. Unlike my mother, who preferred her own grief to raising her son, and my father, who cared too much about himself, Drakos Development gave me something back for the work I put in. The hours I put in, the research, visiting properties, uncovering what it was my sellers coveted and putting their dreams within reach as I netted sale after sale, all of it came back to me. Wealth, prestige, recognition.

It's filled the void left by my parents' neglect. It's been the one thing I've been able to rely on my entire life.

Well, aside from the fact that Lucifer could yank it away at any moment.

"'I, Lucifer Drakos, being of sound mind and body, declare this to be my final will and testament.'"

She starts with Rafe. Aside from inheriting thirty-five percent of Lucifer's shares in Drakos Development, he receives several luxury properties, a substantial monetary inheritance and—oddly—the contents of the library from the villa on Santorini. Our father also includes an edict that Rafe retain his position as head of the European and Asian divisions of Drakos Development.

Something tightens in my chest. He being granted his job in the will is a good sign for me.

But not a guarantee.

Hatred twists in my stomach. I'm fully aware that the last ten years of my life are hanging on the whim of a dying old man who cared only for himself and his bank account.

When Alessandra reads off similar conditions for me, including my keeping my position over the North American offices, the band that's been wrapped around my heart for the past twenty-four years since I learned who my father was loosens. Even Lucifer's death didn't alleviate the tension I've lived with since I was eight years old, standing in the midst of a wealth I couldn't comprehend as a man I'd never met stared down at the child he'd never wanted with disgust.

It's done.

I have my share of Drakos Development.

After Alessandra reads that Michail is inheriting the remaining thirty percent of Lucifer's shares, a couple of

American properties and something about a bequest for Michail's mother, I stop paying attention as I mentally review the upcoming months. Some would find my anticipation of the next steps in my life odd, even inappropriate, in the wake of my father's death. But they wouldn't understand the sense of peace that fills me. The power I now have to make decisions without wondering if it could all be yanked away at any given moment. Now, when I think of my schedule, it's with confidence, excitement. The press conference tomorrow in Malibu to announce the latest West Coast projects. The evaluation of the Mississippi River warehouse development. Then, a meeting in Paris with the board of directors in three weeks.

And after that, I think with a smile, a long weekend. Two or three days in Italy with a woman would be the perfect way to celebrate—

"'As to the conditions…'"

I snap back to the present moment and sit up.

"Conditions?" I repeat.

The vise winds itself back around my chest and tightens until it traps my breath in my lungs. Alessandra looks at me with a glance I can only interpret as apologetic before she resumes reading.

"'I have learned, too late, the value of family. Of legacy. Which is why Rafael, Gavriil, and Michail must marry within one year of the reading of this will and stay married for at least one year, or forfeit everything I have bequeathed to them.'"

CHAPTER TWO

Juliette
Two days later

MY MOM TOOK me to a butterfly garden when I was four. The summer before she died. When we walked into the out-door mesh tent, a swarm of butterflies flew up and around us. Their bodies brushed my skin, their wings soft, their movements frantic.

As I watch people filter into the ballroom, I can feel that same movement now, except it's in my stomach. A flutter of anticipation and determination, underlined with a sharp sliver of doubt.

Anticipation for facing a Drakos once more. Determination to follow through on what might be my last chance to take back my family's legacy.

And doubt. Doubt that's been plaguing me ever since Texas. That's where it first started. I had hesitated in a moment that mattered more than anything else had in my life. Where I came face-to-face with the fact that we are all capable of being monsters.

An ugly, sluggish sensation fills me, drags me down. That doubt has only grown, chipping away at the motivation that had driven my career ever since my first exposé.

When I learned of Lucifer's impending death, my determination dimmed even further, leaving me adrift. That the man I hated more than anything in the world had been part of the foundation of my professional life was a cold truth I hadn't been prepared to confront.

Stop. I'll address my own hang-ups later. Right now, my mission isn't just making sure Lucifer Drakos's cruelty stopped with his death. No, it's a chance to reclaim what he stole from my family fourteen years ago. To give back something to a woman who carved out a piece of heaven for me to live and thrive in even as my life fell apart. Lucifer's death has put that possibility within reach.

If Lucifer's sons and heirs are following in his footsteps and I just happen to uncover another story in the process of achieving my own goals, so be it.

People start filtering into the ballroom. I lean against a pillar, watching, mentally cataloging those in attendance. My initial plan had simply been to observe Gavriil Drakos's press conference, to hear if any of his future plans for the North American division included a certain section of coastline in Washington State.

Specifically, my family's home that Lucifer stole for pennies on the dollar from my reckless father.

The worst part is that, in the years since Lucifer bought Grey House, he visited it once. I saw him arrive in a limo with a tiny blonde woman on his arm. They walked around the property. The wind carried her voice down the hill to where I spied on them from the bushes. I couldn't hear everything, but I heard enough. She wanted a house on the coast, yes, but not in a backwater town that only had two coffee shops and a scattering of restaurants. Never mind that people traveled from all over the world to the peace and quiet elegance of Rêve Beach, or that two of those restaurants had won national awards. All she'd seen was the lack of glitter and, like so many who lived privileged lives, turned her back before she'd truly looked.

I never saw Lucifer at Grey House again. The house was repaired. I watched the new roof being put on, the exterior being sanded and painted.

And then it sat. Empty, lonely, taunting as my father and I squeezed into the tiny gamekeeper's cottage left over from the early days when Grey House had hundreds of acres and a staff that included a butler and a head housekeeper. I watched my father stand at the fence that marks the line between cottage and mansion day after day, pining for what he had lost. His wife. His business. The second woman who loved him even when he couldn't love himself.

By the time I left and moved to Seattle, he had nothing. Nothing but an empty shack and an endless bottle of vodka that served as his only companion when he walked off the edge of a pier and into the cold waters of the Pacific Ocean.

Heat threatens to take over, licking at the edges of my control with a seductive whisper. So tempting to track Gavriil Drakos down, grab him by his tailored collar and vent my fury on him.

But that would accomplish nothing. I'd feel better in the moment, sure. I'd also ruin any chances I have of figuring out if Gavriil knows about Grey House, if he has plans for it or if he might be open to righting his father's wrongs. Not just for my father and myself, but for the woman who had become my second mother. To give her more than a tiny cottage to live out the rest of her life in. A cottage that, when she experiences one of her multiple sclerosis relapses, is impossible for her to navigate in her wheelchair.

Grief rubs against the anger, raw and bleak. The word *stepmother* used to conjure images of the villainess in Cinderella, with her crazy hair and evil cat. But then my father met Dessie three years after my mom passed and I realized that while I would always love my mother, it was possible to love someone else, too. Dessie hadn't pushed her way into my life or ignored me in those early months of her relationship with my dad. She slipped in as much as I would let her, reassuring me when I would feel angry or guilty, stepping back when I needed space.

It's funny how much the little things matter. I walked out one day, late for school, to find a strudel warmed up and waiting for me with my raincoat laid out. It probably took her all of five minutes. But as she looked up and smiled at me from the living room, coffee cup in one hand and our cat Jinx purring on her lap, I realized how well she fit into our lives.

A woman like her deserved the best. Not a man who wasted away after making a colossal mistake. They never married, but she was there, a piece of our lives until my father's desperation and pride drove her out of his life. But not mine. Like clockwork, every other weekend she drove from Seattle to Rêve Beach to see me. When my father could barely take care of himself, let alone his teenage daughter, she stepped in and took me away.

She deserved to have a home of her own. Not the loss of her job that sent her back to Rêve Beach to live with me three years ago. Not a disease that randomly yanks her out of her life for an unknown length of time and, for now, has her living in an assisted-living facility I can barely pay for.

I inhale deeply through my nose, purse my lips, and slowly breathe out. There's far too much at stake for me to give into my emotions. I have to play this carefully. There's nothing illegal about what Lucifer did. He bought the property. He just happened to do it at a fraction of its estimated value, preying on my father's gullibility and desperation as his own business dwindled. It was hideous, horrific.

But not illegal.

Until five years ago when I uncovered something criminal. Not with my father. But someone else. Another victim. One subjected to coercion, force, payouts. I hadn't hesitated then to put together the story that, when it was published a year later, made my career and unveiled Lucifer to the world as the monster he truly was.

A murmur rises as a group of people walk out of a doorway and mount the stage. The first is Rafael Drakos, tall, cold, face sharp like it's been hewn from a glacier. Seeing him—with the same distinct features and icy arrogance as his father—catapults me back to the last time I spoke to Lucifer in person. I'd paid him a visit after he'd stepped back from his role as CEO of Drakos Development amid the fallout. I'd slid my father's picture across the table, knew the moment Lucifer recognized the man he'd conned.

The ice in my spine spreads, fills my veins as I remember the way Lucifer looked at me, eyes dark and lips twisted into a cruel smirk as he offered to sell it back to me at market value. Six times what he had bought it for all those years ago.

Before I'd been able to utter a retort, he'd smiled. "It would be a shame, wouldn't it, to fight me on this? Who knows what might be revealed?"

My father's drinking. His gambling. Grey House meant the world to me. But not enough to sacrifice my father's already tortured memory. To go to court and risk thousands of dollars. I may have won the battle against Lucifer and taken away something he valued. But the war between us was far from over.

Today, though, I have another chance. Unlike five years ago, there's far more at stake. This phase of Dessie's multiple sclerosis has lasted for over a month now. The longest we've ever experienced. We're both wondering the same thing, not wanting to say it out loud. Has the disease progressed? Will she ever have another period of remission again where she can walk without assistance? Live on her own?

Dread builds in my chest as Rafael takes a seat to the side of the podium. I need Grey House. Not, as I once dreamed, to live in, but to sell, to make the kind of money I need for Dessie and me to survive. The thought of it breaks my heart. But I'm out of options. I make decent money as a reporter, but not enough to pay for the care Dessie will need if this is permanent.

As much as I don't care for Rafael and his brooding, superior attitude, he's not my target today.

My gaze shifts to the man moving behind the gleaming podium. Awareness flickers low in my stomach. Broad-shouldered, with mahogany hair and a confident smile he aims like a weapon out over the crowd. Thick head of hair combed back from his face? Check. Square jaw? Check. Chiseled cheekbones I secretly envy? Check. It's not fair for a man like him to be as handsome as he is.

We've interacted over the years, mostly at press conferences. Unlike his father, he's never shied away from my questions or threatened to have me thrown out. As head of the North American division of Drakos Development, he's the most likely holder of Grey House.

The question is, how far does the apple fall from the tree when it comes to Gavriil Drakos? Does he have plans for Grey House? Does he even know it's in his family's roster of holdings? From what I've observed, he's obsessive about details and can quote company facts for days on end. But will a Victorian house on the remote Olympic Peninsula have attracted his attention?

I need to find out if he knows and, if he does, what his plans are so I know what angle to approach him from. Will he do the right thing and pay up the difference of what Grey House was actually worth? Sign it back over to me? Or will I have to go public and unveil a scandal he can't afford as he seeks to show the world he's not like his father?

Our eyes meet. His grin widens, a dare that pisses me off even as it sends an illicit thrill through my veins. I squelch it. I will not be distracted. I will do whatever I have to do to get Grey House back. To provide for Dessie.

I smile back at him. Knocking Gavriil Drakos and his enormous ego down a peg or two is just a bonus.

Gavriil

She stands on the fringes of the ballroom amongst a sea of people, eyes fixed on me with a confident smirk on her lips. Reluctant admiration warms my chest as I arch a brow at her.

Game on, Grey.

I flew from New York to Malibu right after my meeting with Alessandra. Stepping off the plane and into the embrace of the California sunshine did nothing to ease the tension that had slithered under my skin and lay coiled like a snake about to strike ever since learning about Lucifer's ultimatum.

Tension exacerbated by learning that Juliette Grey, the reporter who is the only person in known history to bring my father to his knees, would be in attendance at today's press conference.

I have nothing to hide. But that doesn't mean she hasn't discovered something illicit, something Lucifer did before his death that could bring Drakos Development to the edge once more. I can't think of a single article she's published in the years since her bombshell exposé that didn't include a reference to Drakos Development. Her obsession is the last thing I need to worry about right now, especially when my first priority needs to be finding a wife who will stick with me for a year and satisfy that damned clause.

Unlike the rest of the crowd milling about the ballroom, dressed mostly in name-brand labels and upscale clothing, Juliette is wearing a white T-shirt underneath a cheap-looking gray blazer and simple black pants, with her dark hair pulled up into a ponytail. I rake her casual clothing with my gaze and raise a brow. She returns the gesture and gives me a thumbs-up.

My lips twitch. She's got guts, I'll give her that.

I look away. Confident or not, she's still a threat. I want her to see firsthand how I reassure investors that Drakos Development will not only continue after my father's death, but will flourish.

I do a quick visual sweep of the room. The chandeliers catch the afternoon sunlight filtering in. The massive windows on the far side offer views of the impossibly green grass, soaring palm trees and the Pacific Ocean beyond.

Elegance. Prestige. Wealth. Everything my share of the company embodies.

Selecting the grand ballroom of The Royal for the conference was a good choice. Not only is the Malibu seaside hotel renowned for its opulence, but it was my first success when I ordered the North American branch to break into the hospitality industry. My father called me a foolish bastard.

Literally and figuratively.

I included a bottle of Rémy Martin cognac with the first year's earnings and occupancy report. The handwritten note suggested he pour himself a glass before reading. The old ass never replied, but I didn't need him to. I'd made my point.

Now, with him gone, Rafe and I can finally take the company beyond the selfishness and scandals my father flowed to taint his legacy in his final years.

No longer his legacy. I smile. *Ours.*

Thankfully, Michail wants no part of it. After doing a quick read-up on his company, Sullivan Security, it's clear he has no need for the billions generated every year by our company. He has plenty of his own.

I spare a glance at Rafe standing just to my right. He returns my gaze. Nods. I face the audience, mentally burying my deep-rooted hatred for the man who sired me, and speak.

"Good morning, ladies and gentlemen. It is with profound sadness and yet immense pride that my brother and I stand before you today."

Liar. When Rafe called to tell me the news, I released a pent-up breath. Then I smiled. I kept on smiling as I poured myself a cognac and toasted to his demise. There are plenty who would be shocked by my callousness. Accuse me of being heartless or cold.

They're right. My heart was ripped out twenty-four years ago when my mother died, alone and poor, while my father lived like a king just a few miles away.

I rattle off the speech written for me by someone in Drakos's public relations department. It's drivel, with sappy lines honoring my sire's accomplishments and supposed testimonies from people who knew him. My fingers tighten on the podium every time I say his name.

Anapnéo. I fill my lungs with a deep breath, then slowly release it as I force myself to find a place of calm. This is a minor detour. Right now, my focus needs to be the future of Drakos Development North America.

A future without Lucifer.

With that thought to comfort me, I focus on the microphone.

"Our father's legacy will live on through the continued expansion of Drakos Development."

I finish the maudlin portion of the speech and dive into why I'm really here: my division's growing list of projects along America's West Coast. A buzz whips through the room, feeding my confidence and my ego as I share the three properties I'm most proud of. The three that will mark the beginning of a new era.

"The Serpentine, luxury condos on Catalina Island. The Cooper Industrial Park next to the Port of Los Angeles. The renovation of the Edgware Warehouse Complex in Seattle."

I recite the names and locations from memory as I sweep my gaze over the hotel's grand ballroom. Concept drawings flash on flat screens placed around the room. Appreciative murmurs ripple over the crowd.

My eyes flicker back to the woman leaning against the pillar. Her arms are still crossed, one leg crossed over the other. A casual pose to go with that casual smirk.

But something's changed in the last ten minutes. Her body is no longer relaxed but tight, her shoulders tense beneath her blazer, her pointed chin slightly lifted. Despite her petite stature and huge eyes, she looks anything but innocent. She's been dragging Drakos Development through the mud for years. It's gratifying to see her riled up.

I incline my head in her direction. A deliberate provocation. Instead of glaring or flouncing off, one corner of her mouth curves up. Awareness pricks my skin. I don't like it. Or her. I prefer women soft, warm and willing. Not hard, stubborn, prideful creatures like Juliette Grey.

I face the audience and smile. "Questions?"

Hands shoot up. I answer most of them myself, deferring to Rafe on a couple about our European and Asian markets. The energy in the room is palpable. It fuels me as I smile, laugh and converse with reporters, local legislators and community members.

And then I see it. *Her* hand, slowly easing up, her fingertips waving at me. My first inclination is to ignore her, which annoys the hell out of me. I don't run from a fight. I haven't since I was four. I'm not about to now.

"Miss Grey."

The conversations subside. Most everyone in here knows Juliette. She's made quite the name for herself, appearing on major news networks, podcasts and videos to discuss the results of her investigative reports. She'll disappear for months at a time, only to reappear with a jaw-dropping report on embezzlement, money laundering, fraud, or—my father's specialty—bribery. She's cost companies billions in fines and lost revenue.

Not mine. Not this time.

"First, my condolences on the loss of your father, Mr. Drakos."

Tension tightens my neck. Responding to people's sympathies is hard to do when you have none of your own. But for once, there's no subtle smirk or hidden intention in Juliette's words. She actually appears sincere.

"Thank you," I force out.

"You mentioned several large-scale projects in major metropolitan areas. Any plans for Drakos Development to expand in smaller circles?"

She knows something.

Even from across the ballroom and the few dozen people standing between us, I can feel her emotions. Feel the anticipation, the excitement as she hunts something new.

The problem is, I'm not sure what she's after. None of our plans over the next five years include anything but projects in large cities or tourist destinations.

"Not at this time."

The room seems to hold its collective breath, waiting for her to deliver a customary Juliette Grey follow-up question that will unveil her newest target, wreak havoc or both.

"Thank you."

Surprised, I can only stare as she smiles, nods her head in my direction, and walks out of the ballroom.

Silence reigns for a split second before conversations break out, voices rising as everyone wonders what Juliette's little performance was all about. Many of them cast curious eyes in my direction or, for those with a vested interest in Drakos Development, concerned faces.

I grit my teeth. Perhaps that was her game. To get her name linked to Drakos once again. Put the world on alert that my company was back in her crosshairs.

I don't glance at the door she left through. I'll deal with her later.

Once and for all.

I turn and give the audience a small smile, like I'm letting them in on a little secret.

"Next question?"

CHAPTER THREE

Juliette

SHORTLY AFTER THE press conference adjourns, Gavriil walks out of the ballroom with his brother. I watch them both from a small alcove off to the side and note the similarities and differences between the sons of Lucifer.

The eyes are the same. Both tall, both broad-shouldered. But Rafael's face is sharper, harder, compared to Gavriil's square jaw and quick smile. Gavriil's hair is dark brown compared to Rafael's jet-black, his beard more like a well-groomed shadow. Rafael's is cut to precision. They both command respect, making heads turn as they walk into the main hall.

Gavriil is stopped by a slim blonde woman with a figure shown off to perfection in a navy sheath dress. Natalie, if I remember right. Natalie White, a financial reporter based out of New York. Based on the photos I've seen of Gavriil with his various women over the years, she's just his type.

She throws back her head and laughs as she lays a hand on his arm. He smiles down at her, his teeth flashing white against tan skin. Natalie pulls a card out of a leather folder she's carrying and slips it into the breast pocket of his jacket. He leans down and whispers something in her ear that makes her grin widen and a blush tinge her cheekbones.

An uncomfortable sensation spears through my chest. Being on the shorter side with dark hair and very defined features, I'm the opposite of the blonde and delicate type men like Gavriil and Lucifer prefer. Men don't look at me the way they look at Natalie. It's not something that's bothered me much over the past few years.

But as I watch Gavriil, the charm and focused attention on a woman he finds attractive, I can't deny the envious tug deep in my chest. A tug that turns into a pull as Natalie croons something up at him that makes his smile deepen.

He's a playboy, I reassure myself. *Good-looking, sure. He's also exactly the opposite of what you want or need.*

Natalie gives Gavriil one last steamy glance before walking away. The flirtatious smile disappears as he leans toward Rafael, replaced by an intense focus that hardens his face. They hold a whispered conversation in the middle of the hall. Their bodies are angled just enough that I can't read their lips.

My phone buzzes in my lap. I look down and my stomach drops. An automatic text reminder that Dessie's bill is due. A bill I can make, but just barely, and only because my best friend Catherine is giving me a generous discount. A discount I don't want to accept. But as Catherine lovingly but bluntly reminded me last week, I don't have a choice. And if this relapse continues and turns into secondary-progressive multiple sclerosis, the bills will only continue to climb as Dessie declines.

Unless I can get Grey House back.

I look up just in time to see Gavriil walking toward an arched doorway. I mentally pull up the map of the hotel.

The doorway leads to a flight of stairs that descends to the lower level of the hotel. A heated indoor lap pool, the hotel's spa and a walkout to the cliffside pool.

It takes less than a second for me to make my decision. I had hoped to approach this with more care. Do some additional research, talk to people at Drakos who could give me insight into Gavriil, into any whisperings about Grey House.

You're out of time.

I stand and walk purposefully to the archway. I pass a couple holding hands and a group of women wearing pink sashes on the way down. As I reach the bottom of the stairs, I see Gavriil turning a corner just up ahead. I pass by the glass double doors that lead to the spa and continue. The light dims, overheads giving way to wall sconces covered by aquamarine glass to add a sense of mystique to the white-tiled walls and black floors. Soft music plays from hidden speakers, a slow, deep jazz that lingers over the skin.

I reach the door to the lap pool. I glance back over my shoulder, my senses tingling. There was no other place Gavriil could have gone. I know from my research he's active and usually does something physical at least once a day. But he wasn't carrying a swimsuit or a towel.

I reach into my bag and grab my recorder, flipping it on before I grab the door handle and slowly ease it open. Smooth ivory pillars hold up a mosaic ceiling, the vivid tiles a kaleidoscope of deep blue, glittering gold and alluring red. The lap pool snakes through the floor. Steam rises from the surface. Loungers have been arranged, some at the edge of the pool, others tucked into private alcoves.

I wait, listening, watching. The steam blurs the room,

creating a foggy dreamworld that, coupled with the music drifting on the air, invites one to sit, to relax, to forget.

My fingers tighten around the recorder. A fantasy, nothing more.

After two minutes, there's nothing. No furtive movement, no whispered conversation. My heart sinks. Perhaps I missed a side door. Or perhaps Gavriil continued out to the cliffside pool.

Or maybe you created your own fantasy.

I curse under my breath. Yes, I wanted Gavriil to be up to something. Wanted to find him conducting a clandestine meeting I could record and use to do what I do best.

Bring arrogant bastards to their knees.

I glance around the lap pool room. The last time I stopped to relax was five weeks ago when I met Dessie for a spa day, a break I was so grateful I took when she relapsed just three days later after a fall outside the cottage. Dessie and I opted for matching manicures, and when she chose scarlet, I didn't have the heart to tell her I preferred pale pink or nude. Something that wouldn't draw attention.

I frown down at my nails. The edges are chipped, my real nails showing through at the bottom. I love the idea of indulging in myself more. I just don't have the time.

Neither does Dessie.

My heart catapults into my throat at the thought. I cast one more look over the room. Maybe we could do a road trip in a month if she gets better.

When she gets better, I firmly tell myself.

Take the coastal road and stop off in Crescent City, then continue on down here to Malibu for a long weekend. It would cost more than a penny, sure.

But how much longer does she have?

I swallow my grief and commit to the plan. I click off the recorder and shove it in my pocket as I turn to leave.

Something moves behind me. I start to whirl about, but an arm winds around my waist and yanks me back against a broad chest. Adrenaline kicks in, along with my self-defense training and a healthy dose of fear. I jab my elbow back, but my attacker is quick and strong, only letting out a grunt as I land my blow. Another arm wraps around me just below my breasts, pinning my arms at the elbows.

I open my mouth to scream. The arm around my waist loosens and a split second later a hand slaps over my mouth.

Damn it.

CHAPTER FOUR

Juliette

"RELAX, GREY."

I stop struggling as his voice sinks in. Dark, smooth, laced with his lilting accent.

Gavriil-freaking-Drakos. My body responds to his voice, my heart ticking up as warmth pools in my belly even as my mind snaps at me for letting a spoiled billionaire playboy get the drop on me.

"Are you going to scream?"

His lips brush my ear. I stiffen as the muscles in my thighs clench.

You haven't been on a date in months. Or had sex in... months. I frown as I count back. *Okay, a year and a half. Totally normal reaction.*

I shake my head. His fingers start to loosen, then tighten once more over my jaw.

"I don't know. I rather like it when you can't speak."

Ass.

I force my lips open and graze my teeth against his palm, a threat of what I'm willing to do. The action startles him enough that he loosens his grip. I sag in his arms. He swears and stumbles backward. I lean forward, breaking his hold, and then whirl around to face him.

"Don't ever sneak up on me or touch me without my permission," I snap.

He rights himself and stares me down. He's nearly a foot taller than me. Steam swirls around him. With the dim lighting and his dark suit, he looks like a demon lying in wait.

I reach into my pocket and hit the button on my recorder.

"You're the one who followed me, Grey."

"Which I think you wanted, Mr. Drakos."

He arches a brow, the one with a small scar bisecting the dark hair. "Oh?"

"Or perhaps I interrupted an assignation?" I smile sweetly at him. "Is Natalie White joining you?"

His lips curve up. "Jealous, Grey?"

I manage not to snarl at him. "I don't have any interest in another woman's leftovers."

His amusement disappears as his mouth flattens into a grim line. "Keep your speculations about my private life out of your gossip rag."

That he didn't deny a personal relationship with Natalie bothers me for reasons I don't care to examine. That he calls my work *gossip* infuriates me to the point I almost lose focus and lash out.

Stay on target.

"Gossip implies the facts have not been verified, Mr. Drakos. I always verify."

"And ruin people's lives in the process."

Men like Gavriil have no idea what *ruin* means to the average person. Have no idea about the children left behind, the women with broken hearts, the families without a penny to their name. All they care about is their own wealth, their reputations.

"I'm not in the business of ruining people. I reveal them for who they really are."

"Then you should know that my brother and I are not like my father."

He's got me there. In all my research on the Drakos men, I found little to suggest that Rafael and Gavriil were close with Lucifer. The subtle venom in Gavriil's voice makes me wonder what happened before he grew up, those early years that are still a mystery. If there's something there that can be used to further my cause.

However, as I've learned the hard way, the words that come out of someone's mouth, the expressions of grief or outrage or sympathy, all of it can be twisted, manipulated. I've talked with Gavriil less than a dozen times over the years, all in a professional capacity. I don't know him nearly well enough to know if he's lying right now. If his supposed disgust of his father is real or an act.

"We'll see."

Gavriil's eyes narrow to slits. "The man was cruel, arrogant and greedy."

"Agreed."

"And I don't begrudge the first story you published about him."

I blink in surprise. "You read it."

"It was well researched. Lucifer was wrong."

I mentally note his use of his father's first name.

"He threatened and harassed an eighty-year-old grandmother of seven into nearly selling her property for a fraction of its worth, or face having her house condemned by the county."

His jaw tightens. "Like I said. He was wrong."

I tilt my chin up. "What if you found out you and your brother were now in possession of property that had been obtained in a similar manner?"

He moves before I can blink, stopping with mere inches between us. My breath catches in my chest as I look up. I try to keep my face professional, try not to let this man see the physical effect he has on me. It would give him power over me. Power I have no doubt he would use to get what he wants.

But it also irritates me. I've never been the type to fall for a handsome face. I'm not about to start now with the son of the man who ruined my family.

"What do you know, Grey?"

"I know a lot of things."

He leans down. *Damn it.* I take a step back, not wanting to let him get *too* close. But it's too late. That sensual awareness that I felt back in the ballroom slams back into my body and curls through me, leaving me breathless and unfocused as my gaze lands on his mouth.

My back hits the wall. His hands come up on either side, pinning me in.

"You know something about one of the properties."

I cock my head to one side, faking a bravado I don't feel as my pulse pounds even as my mind screams at me to slow down, to not let lust get in the way of what I need to do. I inhale, acutely aware of the barest brush of my breasts against his chest. His eyes flare as his lips part slightly.

Focus!

I mentally reach out and manage to rein in my racing thoughts. Judging by the underlying question in what he just said, the balance has just tipped in my favor. He doesn't like the idea that I might hold some knowledge of his father's illicit doings over his head. Maybe even fears it.

"Yes."

"What did he do?"

The rawness in his voice catches my attention. Gone is the silver-tongued heir who dominated the podium in the ballroom. Standing before me is a man who knows the truth about the man who fathered him. A man who, judging by the pain and fury in his blue eyes, is tortured by that knowledge.

I never thought I'd feel a kinship with Gavriil Drakos. Every time I've seen him, talked to him, he's come across like an arrogant jerk who knows he's handsome and wealthy and could care less about what his father's done.

But right now, as he stares down at me, our breaths mingling with the steam and creating shapes out of shadows, I realize how much this man is hurting. Hurting because of decisions made by someone else.

The truth hits me. He doesn't know about Grey House. Knows nothing about Simon Jones, his wife, or the woman he later loved. His daughter. And I'm using his lack of knowledge, his embarrassment over his father, to get what I want.

Shame weighs down my heart. I'm doing what so many have done before me. What I promised myself I would never do, especially after Texas. Even knowing there's a purpose to it doesn't make me feel any less ugly inside. Doesn't stop the knife that was shoved into my conscience all those months ago from twisting a little deeper.

"I don't think here is the place—"

"Cut the crap, Grey."

I blink. "Excuse me?"

"You know something. What are you planning?" He leans down further. "Blackmail?"

My empathy evaporates. I curl my fingers into my palms, the nails digging into my skin, to stop myself from slapping him across the face.

"Blackmail was your father's specialty, not mine."

"Don't think for a second you can drag Rafe or me down with him."

I stand up on my toes, bringing our lips within a breath of each other's. Do I imagine his sharp intake of breath? Probably. Despite our moment of attraction earlier, men like him prefer women like Natalie White. Glamorous, fair, voluptuous. Not short, skinny, nosy reporters who have exposed his family's secrets for the world to see.

"If you have nothing to hide, then you have nothing to worry about."

His hands come up and grab my shoulders. The heat from his palms seeps into my skin. "I do worry. I worry far too much about you, Grey."

Shocked, and more aroused than I've been in…well, ever, I swallow hard. His touch is possessive, his fingers searing my body through the material of my blazer. A brand. It should disgust me. I should be bringing my knee up and ramming it into his groin. The man is arrogant, rude, conceited and a Drakos.

But I don't. I don't because for one moment, I'm not thinking about revenge or illness or the depths of human depravity. I'm savoring how it feels to be wanted, desired. Indulging in a yearning I've never experienced before with a man who tests the limits of my patience even as he has earned my grudging respect for doing what his father never had the courage to do and go head-to-head with me.

Carnal images fill my mind, remnants of dreams I've suppressed and imaginings that make me blush even as they make me crave. It takes my very limited reserves of self-control to stop myself from rising up on my toes and pressing my mouth to his.

He lowers his head. God, I can feel his breath against my lips.

Just a taste.

A sharp peal of muted laughter sounds off to my right. A moment later the door swings open. The women in pink sashes stream through, still wearing the sashes but now sporting swimwear. A couple of them cast glances at Gavriil and me. Some keep their eyes focused on him, not bothering to hide their appreciation of his impressive physique. Others shoot me an envious glance. One even winks at me and gives me a thumbs-up.

Gavriil releases me and steps back, nodding to the passing women with a smile that could kill. They titter and preen as they head toward the first set of lounge chairs clustered at the edge of the lap pool.

That uncomfortable feeling when I saw him with Natalie hits again, harder and deeper after our intimate moment. I did what I haven't done since I started my career—I let myself be swayed by a handsome face. Whether he was genuinely attracted to me moments ago or was just faking his response to distract me, I don't know. But his ability to step away so quickly, to smile at another woman like she's the best thing he's seen all day seconds after nearly kissing me, reinforces the rule I almost forgot.

Men like Gavriil—like Lucifer—don't care about other people.

Be careful, sweetheart, I can hear Dessie murmuring as

she brushed my hair before a school dance. He turns his back to me, the smile disappearing as it's replaced by a dark brooding that sends a shiver down my spine. *A handsome face can hide an ugly heart.*

"Goodbye, Mr. Drakos."

His eyes harden as he starts to reply.

"If she's turning you down, I'm free, sexy!" one of the women calls from the edge of the pool. "I could use a date for the wedding tonight." The women around her alternate between laughter and groans.

I shoot her a grin over his shoulder. "He's all yours. And I've heard he loves to dance."

He glares daggers at me. The sight boosts my mood and I incline my head. "Mr. Drakos."

"This isn't over, Grey. Not by a long shot."

"On that, Mr. Drakos, we agree."

I leave the pool, walk past the spa, and ascend the stairs, my body tense as I listen for the sound of footsteps behind me.

Nothing. He's letting me go.

Good.

I reach the main floor of the hotel.

Time to regroup. Strategize.

The next meeting will be in an office setting, preferably one of my choosing. I'll have research, notes, everything I need to make my case.

That and an iron grip on my wayward desire. He didn't even hesitate to shut down his reaction to me when the bridal party came in, to engage in flirtation with another woman as if we hadn't just been about to tear each other's clothes off.

It hurts. My throat tightens as I hit the top of the stairs. It hurts and I hate that it hurts. That I let myself be swayed for even a moment by the chemistry between us. Even though I tell myself I won't let things go that far again, I make a promise as I move toward the main doors of the hotel to never let myself get that close to him again, especially in a dark room that blurs my inhibitions and tempts me to the edge of reason.

No matter how much I might fantasize otherwise.

CHAPTER FIVE

Gavriil

I STARE AT the storm-lashed beach from the driver's seat of my convertible. Rain drums on the leather roof. It's thin enough I can see the sea, steely gray waves churned white in places by nature's fury.

My fingers tighten on the wheel. I know the feeling.

Why, of all places, my father decided to steal a house from a tour boat operator on the coast of Washington State is beyond me. The sand here is dark. Pine, fir and spruce trees cover the craggy mountains, casting shadows. As soon as I arrived in Seattle, I was met with rain.

That was nearly three hours ago.

My glance slides from the gloomy landscape to the house just beyond my car. It sits on a bluff with a good view of the ocean. Architecturally speaking, it's beautiful. A Victorian manor painted dove gray with dramatic touches like a wraparound porch, tall arched windows on all three floors and at least two towers I can see from this angle. The lawn surrounding the house is lush green and trimmed.

I have a hard time believing Juliette would care for the house like this. She's methodical in her work. But she's also brash, bold. If the house was hers, I'd expect overflowing flowerpots with no rhyme or reason to the blooms, and the siding painted in a bright shade as if to let the whole world know she was there. Organized chaos.

Which leaves me with the ugly conclusion that Lucifer maintained the house to this level of immaculate perfection simply to taunt Juliette that it was no longer hers.

I breathe in. What I'm about to do could cement my future. Ensure Drakos Development survives while also taking care of one pesky reporter. All good things. Doesn't mean I don't feel like I'm about to sentence myself to hell.

Proposing to one's sworn enemy tends to do that.

It was Juliette who gave me the idea. When she deserted me at the pool with lust pounding through me like a sledgehammer and the single bridesmaid—who I swear licked her lips as she batted her eyes at me—her last words had crawled under my skin.

I'm not the kind of girl a guy like him goes for. And, she'd added with that brazen smile I couldn't get out of my head, *vice versa*.

I'd gone to my suite that night alone with the weight of Juliette's insinuations pressing on my chest. That and a throbbing need to fill myself with her, to tug at the ties pulling back her hair and watch it tumble free around her shoulders before I buried my fingers in it. To taste her skin as I drove myself inside her. I'd stroked myself in the shower that night, and the morning after, to rid myself of the desire that had sunk its claws into me. Even after giving myself a release, it hadn't fully taken the edge off.

So I'd changed my focus and turned to business. Starting with a thorough investigation into Juliette. I'd anticipated creating a stronger foundation for myself as I tried to figure out what hold she might have over me. I hadn't foreseen the shocking ties she had to Lucifer, or how far back her connection to Drakos Development went.

I'd sat on my private balcony twenty-four hours after the press conference, golden sand just beyond the railing and rich blue ocean past that, with a brandy in one hand and my tablet in the other as I read through the report provided to me by the private investigator I kept on retainer. Knowing the deepest secrets of my business associates—and my enemies—had come in handy more than once.

As it had this time. Learning that Juliette's first report on Lucifer had been based on a vendetta dating back to her childhood instead of the good girl persona she presented to the world had been deeply satisfying. She'd always struck me as black-and-white. But she had her own shades of gray layered beneath her confidence. A complexity I couldn't help but find intriguing. Coupled with how much willpower it had taken not to kiss her in the spa, she had become something of an obsession. A threat, yes, but also a mystery to unravel.

My lips curl back from my teeth in a snarl. I have no need to know her on a deeper level. Don't need the temptation that offers, especially when I've woken up the past three mornings with the scent of her filling my head and my fingers burning from the memory of her skin beneath my touch. Yes, she's sexy and complex, more than just a damned moral crusader fighting against her so-called villains.

But I don't care. I don't care about her reasons. I don't care about her backstory. The only thing that matters is getting her to agree to be my wife, stay married for a year, and then go on her merry way. The snarl smooths into a smirk as I think about how her name will forever be tied to mine, even after the divorce. Even if she chooses to target Drakos Development in the future, any stories will be easily dismissed as the bitter writings of an ex-wife.

I get out and walk quickly through the cold rain to the cover of the porch. I glance down at my watch. Thirty minutes until she'll be here. I texted her last night requesting a meeting and included the address. Nearly an hour had passed before I received her one-word reply: Fine.

It had been deeply satisfying to picture her face, brows raised in shock, eyes narrowed in anger at me figuring everything out. I'd held on to that image throughout my trip, especially the long drive from civilization to the middle of nowhere.

I walk up and down the length of the porch. A quick glance into the windows confirms the rooms are devoid of furniture, but the flooring has recently been stained a dark gray. White trim gleams despite the shadow of the storm. I start to pull the key out of my pocket. The drumming of rain on the porch roof softens. I turn to see it abruptly give way to a light mist. Despite my preference for sun and warmth, the effect is not unpleasant.

Curiosity drives me down the steps and out onto the wet lawn. I circle around the house. There's a veranda off the back that overlooks the ocean. Empty garden beds sprawl across the backyard, a defiant plant pushing up through the soil here and there.

In my mind's eye, I can picture the house as it could be. Gardens lush with native plants that would thrive in the wet, cooler climate. The veranda dotted with cozy chairs and subtle lighting for the darker days. Still not my preferred setting. But it could be a nice one.

Still doesn't answer the question of why. Why my father

snatched this property away from one Simon Jones, father of Juliette Grey. Why he kept the house maintained, at least on the outside, but did absolutely nothing with it.

But Lucifer never did need a valid reason to indulge his cruel nature. It could be as simple as Simon bragged about his house and Lucifer decided he had to have it. Like a spoiled child who always wants what others have. Never satisfied.

I move past the gardens toward the cliff. A wooden fence runs the length of the property on the south side of the lawn, marked by a small gate. The plateau the house sits on slopes down at the fence line. The hill is fairly steep and falls out of sight. But I can still spy a glimpse of a roof at the bottom.

A roof of a cottage that, way back when, belonged to a gamekeeper back when Grey House presided over hundreds of acres. A cottage that now belongs to Juliette.

Not liking the sudden uptick in my heartbeat, I turn away from the sight of the cottage and focus on the ocean. No reason to be on edge. She had the upper hand back in Malibu. She knew it, and I can't help but respect her for how she played it. But the tide has turned, and I'm back in control once more.

Satisfaction heats my blood despite the brisk wind pulling at my coat. Juliette is the key I need to move forward, to be free from Lucifer's hold once and for all and ensure Drakos Development's success for decades to come.

I won't leave until my ring is on her finger.

I stop within a dozen feet of the cliff. The sea has settled, the waves still choppy and capped with white, but smoother, more graceful. The mix of pine and evergreen trees covering the slopes shift from craggy and peculiar to regal as the fog abates. Further down the coast to my right is the small town of Rêve Beach. A cluster of houses, shops, wineries, cafés and restaurants, with a luxury resort and a couple small hotels. Not my idea of a vacation enclave, but my research showed it did well enough.

It's where Simon Jones ran a tour boat that had brought in a modest income until a year before my father bought Grey House. That was when his finances took a nosedive as the occasional sports bet had turned into reckless gambling. He took out a second mortgage on the house at an exorbitant rate, sold his business, and then finally sold the house.

Three months later, he was found dead in a rock-strewn cove near the north end of town.

I eye the edge of the cliff, the sharp drop-off. The dark beach lies sequestered at the bottom. The coroner's report had included suspicions of suicide. But with witnesses testifying that Simon had imbibed far too much at a local bar before insisting he could walk home himself during a rainstorm, it had officially been ruled an accident. The life insurance, a mere twenty-five thousand dollars taken out four weeks before his death, had been bequeathed to his only child. A child who had disappeared off the face of the earth for the next four years, until she'd reappeared as Juliette Grey at a university in Missouri renowned for its journalism program.

When I first read the report, sympathy snuck in. I know what's it like to lose a parent as a child. Juliette had been six years older than I was when my mother passed. But still a child, one who had lost a mother at the age of five and then her father less than a decade after that.

Had she gone to live with family? Been put into the foster system? I hadn't dug too deep on that score. It had been irrelevant to my initial goals. But now the questions poked me. I'd learned so much about her in the past two days. The missing gaps added to the mystery of the woman who dared to spar with me, who had driven me to a level of sexual frustration I hadn't experienced in…well, ever.

Yet there is still so much I don't know. I had respected her for years as a reporter, then loathed her for the exact same reason. She is a paradox.

And that, I remind myself as I take one last look at the sea, is what I need to keep in mind. There's nothing special about her. When she says yes to my proposal, we'll spend time together as needed. But there will be no more intimate settings that threaten my control. No more near-kisses that torment me. Gradually, the mystery of Juliette will give way to familiarity, which will lead to indifference and apathy. The traditional cycle of many a relationship.

Awareness prickles over my skin. I glance to my left and she's there at the gate. I wondered if she would show up early, perhaps even be lying in wait on the porch.

My thoughts dissipate as a gust of wind catches the long dark hair she normally wears in a bun and pulls tendrils over her face. She doesn't brush them aside. No, she simply stands there, strong and impervious, watching me.

My gaze slides over her. It's not just the hair that's different. She's wearing a dress underneath a tan shawl, a long-sleeved burgundy gown that hugs her slender torso. With a heart-shaped neckline and little buttons between her breasts, it softens her, makes her look both fierce and feminine.

A combination I respond to as my body tightens. A warning whispers in my mind. The attraction that surged between us in the grotto was unexpected. So, too, is this side of her I've never seen.

But then I remember the late-night call from a buyer after her article went live. The frantic flurry of emails from my public relations department. The sidelong glance cast my way by an investor. All of my hard work threatened by a few words from this woman.

My lips tilt up. Not only will my proposal solve multiple problems, it will also be incredibly satisfying. I can handle an aggravating attraction if it means her silence with a side of retribution.

"Good morning, Miss Grey," I call out.

"It would be a better one if you weren't here."

I can't help the smile that crosses my face.

"Tell me how you really feel."

She cocks her head to one side. "You know."

"I do."

She doesn't reply, simply watches me.

"Are you keeping your distance so you don't give in to the urge to strangle me?"

"This is your land. I don't want to trespass."

She states it matter-of-factly. So succinctly I nearly miss the glint in her eyes, the edge to her words.

"It used to be yours."

"Used to. Now it's not."

Her gaze shifts to the right. Longing flits across her face. Even as I experience the quick thrill of knowing my proposal will be an easy sell, I can't dismiss the uncomfortable sensation of empathy. I know what it's like to be within reach of what you want. To see it day after day, thinking that perhaps tomorrow you will finally have it within your grasp.

I can give Juliette what she wants. I'm good at giving people what they want. A talent born from being denied what I wanted for so long. I cling to that thought and dismiss the sliver of guilt that's slipped beneath my skin and rests there, small but sharp.

"You went after my father because of what he did to yours."

"Initially." One eyebrow quirks up. "He provided more than enough reasons for me to keep an eye on him."

Satisfied at hearing her confirm my suspicions, I move toward her with measured steps. She doesn't back down. No, instead she squares her shoulders, her body tensing as if bracing for me to push her away from the gate.

"He set you on the path to becoming a reporter."

Her face darkens.

"I became a reporter because it's what I wanted to be."

"Touché. And because you're a good reporter, you know I am nothing like my father."

She tilts her head as she regards me, a Mona Lisa smile touching her lips. "I know there's no evidence of bribery, coercion or extortion."

Some of my good humor evaporates, replaced by quiet anger.

"But?"

"But you're still relentless. Borderline ruthless."

"The same could be said of you."

Darkness flares in her eyes, a sorrow that speaks to something deep inside me buried beneath years of pain. Then it's gone and she raises her chin up in the air.

"Perhaps. But pair those qualities with astronomical wealth, good looks, and a silver tongue, and you have the conditions for a man who could be very dangerous."

I smile. "You think I'm good-looking."

That brow shoots up again. "You know you are."

The wind kicks up over the edge of the cliff, gentler this time as the storm continues on its path just north of us. A stray lock of hair drifts across her cheek. I mentally curl my fingers back into my palm to stop my first inclination of reaching up to smooth the strand away.

"So you're prejudiced against handsome, wealthy men."

"Wary. Given my history, as you've discovered," she says with a nod to the house behind me, "you can understand why."

"I can understand why you had an aversion to my father."

"Him. Damian Ruthford. Alfonso Adams. Peter Walter."

She steps forward until she's pressed against the gate. Damn it, I don't want to like her. But my esteem for her climbs up as she says the names of the men she's brought to their knees with the power of her pen.

"Yes, Mr. Drakos. I have an aversion. An aversion to men who abuse their wealth and power and leave nothing but suffering in their wake."

I hear it, the slight catch in her voice.

"How did you suffer, Grey?"

Her throat moves as she swallows. Her eyes flick once more to the house, then back to me. All trace of yearning disappears as she meets my gaze.

"I didn't suffer. I grew stronger."

It's not just respect that fills my chest. Not just lust that lurks in my veins. No, it's recognition. Like me, Juliette faced down the impossible at a young age. We could have surrendered to our losses, our grief. But instead of letting it beat her, she fought back. We combatted instability, uncertainty, and rose to achieve our own forms of success. To carve out our places in the world and take pride in the roles we created.

I look back at the house. A few beams of watery sunlight break through the clouds to touch the fresh paint, making the railing of one of the second-floor balconies gleam white.

"You grew up here."

"The house was in my mother's family for five generations."

"Grey House." I glance around. "Aptly named."

"Not everything has to be glittering gold."

I turn back to see her look across the sea. Her face softens into a smile that makes my body tighten. These glimpses of the woman behind the reporter are unnerving. I can handle her determination, her confidence, even the attraction that sizzles between us, no matter how strong it may be.

But the softness…that's a different beast. One that beckons, invites me to give in to that temptation to unravel the mystery of who this woman is, to get to know her better.

I don't want that closeness. Not with her. Not with anyone.

"There's beauty in everything." She nods toward the retreating clouds. "Even storms."

I think back to another storm, one where cold rain poured in through cracks around the window as I curled against my mother's side, listening to the death rattle in her chest as she gasped for air between bursts of thunder.

"Not everything."

Her head snaps back to me and the softness disappears, thank God.

"Did you just come to make conversation, or are you here for a reason?"

"I'm here to propose a mutually beneficial arrangement." I smile at her again, the smile I wield before I offer people what they desire. "One that would include me signing over the deed to Grey House."

Even the air seems to still as she stares at me. Then she inhales sharply and time resumes. Her lips part as her eyes move between the house and me.

"What price are you asking?"

"A reasonable and affordable one."

I reach into my pocket and pull out a black velvet box. The confusion on her face would be amusing if so much didn't hinge on her saying one specific word.

"What…"

Her voice trails off as I flip open the lid to reveal a ten-carat diamond set into a platinum band decorated with smaller, but no less fine, diamonds.

"Your hand in marriage."

CHAPTER SIX

Juliette

THIS HAS TO be a joke. There is no scenario in this universe where Gavriil Drakos would propose to me.

I stare at the ring. It's so opulent it's almost comical.

"Is that fake?"

Gavriil glares at me.

"It's a million-dollar ring, Grey."

I'd laugh at the offense in his tone if I wasn't still shell-shocked.

"Is there a hidden camera somewhere?" I look around. We appear to be alone on the bluff, but Gavriil could have easily paid for cameras to be secreted around the property. "Is this some elaborate prank to embarrass me? Punish me for looking into your family?"

He frowns at me like I'm an idiot.

"It's a proposal, Grey. I'm asking you to marry me."

"Why on earth would you want to marry me?"

He gives me a lazy smile, which stirs some of the warmth that's lingered ever since our near-kiss in the grotto. I hate that he has that effect on me.

"I don't want to marry anyone. But I have to."

"Come again?"

He sighs. "We may not see eye to eye on some things, Grey. But on the subject of my father, we can both agree he was a bastard." His lips twist into something menacing that makes my chest clench. The fury flickering in his eyes as he snaps the lid shut on the ring box gives me far deeper insight into just why he's so successful at what he does than any research I could have done. For all his pomp and flash, Gavriil Drakos has a dark side. One that sends a not unpleasant shiver down my spine as I see a glimpse of the dominant leader behind the mask of amused arrogance he so often shows to the world.

"I shared at the press conference that Rafael and I inherited our shares of Drakos Development. What I neglected to mention was that inheritance is contingent upon my marrying and staying married for a year."

My jaw drops.

"What?"

The snarl disappears as the amused glint I'm used to reappears.

"I had similar, if not more colorful sentiments, when I learned about it three days ago."

"What happens if you don't get married?"

The fury returns, hardening his face as his fingers curl around the ring box like he might crush the diamond in his grasp.

"Then I lose everything."

It sounds absurd, like the plot of one of the cheesy yet swoon-worthy romance novels I read when I have time. Yet the stunning viciousness of it is what hits me hardest of all. I know firsthand how malicious and selfish Lucifer could be. But to hear he inflicted that emotional brutality on his own sons makes my heart ache for the seemingly impervious man standing in front of me.

"That's sick."

One thick brow curves up. "On that we can agree."

"What's the purpose? Did he doubt your ability to lead?"

He glances over his shoulder at Grey House. "You know how cruel and capricious he was. Did he need a reason to torment his sons from beyond the grave?"

There's a story there, seething beneath his supposed apathy. A story that, for once, I want nothing to do with as I shove away my sympathy once more. I don't want this personal detail of his life. I don't want to see the pain of his childhood, to feel sympathy for him.

But why?

The question passes through my mind and freezes me in place. Why am I so determined to believe the worst of Gavriil and Rafael Drakos? Because they're related to the man who ruined my father's life? Because they're wealthy? I was furious when Gavriil accused me of being prejudiced against rich people.

Except…he's right. I've spent my career exposing the lies and hypocrisies of the rich and powerful. I've dedicated my life to ripping the masks off predators who hide behind money and power. But now…now I'm wondering if I've gone too far. Focused so hard on the people I'm chasing that I've been blind to the innocent people between myself and my own goals. People like Gavriil, who might be an arrogant bastard, but who is nothing like the man who fathered him.

Gavriil is offering me what I've wanted ever since Lucifer stole it: Grey House. More than that, he's offering me a chance to help Dessie, to secure the future she deserves even if he doesn't seem to know about the woman who held my life together.

Except this choice isn't as black-and-white as the first one I made when embarking on this journey—to reveal Lucifer for who he really was to the world and ensure he could never hurt an innocent person ever again. This choice is layered with pitfalls, such as sacrificing my integrity as I marry a man whose values center on the two things I detest the most: money and power.

One year ago, the answer would have been simple. No matter how badly I wanted Grey House, it wouldn't have been worth it.

But now, it's not just about me. And as I stare at the familiar pillars and turrets of the home I grew up in, I also know that the career I've poured my heart and soul into is no longer the driving force behind my existence.

It's a punch to the gut. One that leaves me breathless and adrift.

"So?"

I blink and refocus on Gavriil.

"So what?"

He holds up the ring. The massive stone glints in the weak sunlight fighting through the clouds. It looks nothing like a ring I would wear. Ostentatious, over-the-top. Even if Gavriil is nothing but a brazen billionaire, his preference for the finer things in life is off-putting.

"Why are you asking me? We don't even like each other."

He splays a hand on his chest.

"You wound me, Grey."

"With what? Honesty?"

He chuckles. The sound is surprisingly warm, deep. It rolls through me, leaving a trail of wanting in its wake.

My hands tighten on the gate. The wet wood is a necessary contrast to the heat I can't seem to get rid of since our
encounter in the spa. That heartbeat of a moment where I
felt beautiful and sexy and desired.

"This has nothing to do with liking or attraction. It's a
practical decision."

"For two people who don't like each other to get married
to satisfy the requirements of an asinine clause?"

"I have something you want."

I can't help it, can't stop my eyes from drifting over his
shoulder to Grey House. When I came back after I gradu-
ated college and took up residence in the cottage, it had
nearly killed me to see the house every day. To remember
which window I sat at with my mother when a winter storm
lashed the town. To close my eyes and envision sitting on
the balcony off my parents' room as spring drifted in and
warmed the wood beneath me. Aside from Dessie, it's the
one thing I have left of my family, my childhood.

And now it's within reach. But Gavriil lied. The price is
not reasonable. A year with him is a very steep cost.

"I'm sure there are any number of women who want
something you could give them."

"True. But none of them have something I want, too."

My skin grows cold beneath the warmth of my wrap as
his grin flashes white.

"Which is?"

"Your name on a contract swearing you'll never write a
poisonous word about Drakos Development again, or you'll
forfeit ownership of Grey House back to me."

I rear back before I can stop myself. I knew there had
to be more to this proposal. Hearing him state it out loud,

as casually as if we were discussing the weather, infuriates me.

"You're trying to bribe me."

"No. I'm offering an incentive."

"You're splitting hairs, Drakos," I spit out.

"Call it what you want, Grey." The amusement vanishes, replaced by the steely-eyed businessman I've heard so much about but never witnessed firsthand. "We both know your research for the past four years has revealed no wrongdoing on my part. You have nothing but a vendetta against my father, driving this relentless campaign against my family. The fact that I have to offer you anything to get you to back off and leave us alone is a testament to your lack of professionalism."

My lips part in shock. I flounder for a moment as his words stab straight into the heart of my doubts and insecurities.

His smile returns, but his eyes remain hard.

"So accept my offer. Live a life of luxury and glamour. Give your pen a break. Move back into your childhood home." He looks back over his shoulder. "You've wanted it for years. It can be yours again."

I bite my tongue. I'd heard rumors and firsthand accounts of what made Gavriil so good at what he did. The man has a knack for identifying people's deepest desires and then making them happen. Easy to do when so many want money, or something money can buy them, and he has it in abundance.

I never would have thought myself capable of accepting any deal. But...

"What's holding you back?"

His voice is silky now, dark and tempting. I avoid his

gaze as I stare at the familiar pillars and curves of Grey House. I can't tell him what's truly holding me back. I don't want to share that fear is making me pause: Fear that he's right and I'm incapable of letting go of my vendetta. Fear that if I accept his offer, I'm giving in to someone who may not be the monster I imagined him to be, but still represents so much of what I don't like about this world. Fear that if I don't, I'll never have another chance like this to solidify Dessie's future.

My phone buzzes in my pocket. I pull it out and stifle a groan. My alarm reminding me about the social at Dessie's facility. Catherine told me Dessie's been sleeping more and more. Each day that passes when she can barely get out of bed, when her legs collapse beneath her and she won't use the walker or wheelchair, spikes my fear higher and higher that she won't come back from this.

Dessie...

My eyes snap back to the house. An idea appears. One that is most definitely selfish, as it will give me something I want even as it solves my most pressing problem. But one that also gives me back some of the control I've lost.

"Will this be in name only?"

A corner of his mouth twitches. "No sex required."

It shouldn't bother me how easily he agrees to no sex.

Whatever.

"Then I agree."

I detest the satisfied smile that spreads across his face.

"I'll have my lawyers—"

"I agree," I repeat, "for Grey House and two million dollars, payable before the wedding."

The smile disappears. Any satisfaction I would have derived from it is eclipsed by the icy cold that stills his features. I can feel the disapproval emanating from him as much as I can feel the renewed wind sweeping up from the sea.

"Everyone has their price." He cocks his head to the side. "I didn't expect yours to be so mercenary."

I think of Grey House. I think of Dessie sitting on the patio in the summer with a raised garden bed that will accommodate her wheelchair if her prognosis worsens. I think of turning the empty guest bedroom into an office where I can work. Of not having to worry about money ever again, no matter what hurdles Dessie's condition may throw in our path.

These are the thoughts that keep me from smacking the judgmental look off Gavriil Drakos's handsome face. He may not be a criminal like his father. But he is a selfish creature who has no problems enjoying his own wealth even as he judges others for wanting a better life for themselves and the ones they love.

"Do we have a deal?"

He stares at me for one long second before nodding. I stick out my hand.

"Oh, no." His eyes gleam. "A deal of this magnitude requires something more than a handshake."

He flips the lid open on the ring box and takes the ring out before he grabs my left hand. I freeze as his fingertips warm my skin, barely hold back a shiver as he slides the ring on. It's cold. Feels more like a shackle than the most expensive piece of jewelry I've ever worn.

"What happens now?" I ask as I cross my arms over my chest.

"Now you plan the wedding of the century."

My jaw drops.

"What?"

"We have to convince the world that, after years of acrimony, we're suddenly in love and desperate to get married."

My brilliant idea now sounds brilliantly stupid as I stare at the man I've just bound myself to for a year. I thought we'd take care of this quickly and quietly: a simple ceremony, sign our names, then live out the rest of our sentence separately.

"Why not just go to the courthouse—"

"No."

"Why not?" I ask, not bothering to hide the frustration from my voice.

"It's not my style."

"What if it's mine?"

"My offer, my rules. Two," he continues, his voice hardening, "there is to be no hint, not even a whisper, of the real reason for our wedding."

"I take it I'll be signing more than just a marriage license," I reply dryly.

"An ironclad nondisclosure with the condition you'll forfeit anything I grant you if you end the marriage early or tell anyone about the will."

"What if I pinky promise?"

The brooding scowl disappears as he throws his head back and laughs. A deep, rich laugh that makes my skin tingle with the pleasantness of the sound.

"I don't think that counts as legally binding."

I sigh and wrap my arms tighter around myself, partly to ward off the lingering chill and partly to comfort myself.

"So you're wanting this…circus to convince people we're marrying because we love each other?"

"That's part of it. No one who knows me would expect

me to go to a courthouse. And," he adds with a wicked grin, "there's something satisfying about having you play the role of blushing bride."

I roll my eyes, then curse as my phone vibrates again.

"I have to go."

"I'm staying at the Seaside Inn through tomorrow morning. I'll have my lawyers fax over the paperwork." He reaches out and catches my arm as I start to turn away. "Come by later and I'll have the hotel print them off for you to sign."

"I'm busy tonight. Maybe tomorrow."

His body tenses.

"Busy doing what?"

I tug my arm away, not caring for his tone. "Busy doing something I already had scheduled before you decided to invade my home and bribe me."

"I neglected to mention that dating or seeing anyone else is off-limits until our divorce is finalized."

"Is that a two-way street?" I snap.

An image appears in my head, vivid and unbidden, of Gavriil rolling around naked in bed with some tall, glamorous model. It's an extremely unpleasant vision.

Not because I'm jealous, I reassure myself.

"Adultery is not a habit I indulge in."

Dear God, he almost sounds offended. Right after he just insinuated that I would be entertaining men on the side during the course of our so-called marriage.

"No," I reply with a sweet smile, "just a new woman every week."

He returns my smile with a slow curving of his full lips that draws my attention down to his mouth before snapping my eyes back up to his amused gaze.

"Jealous again, Grey?"

"Nothing to be jealous over. We're not in a relationship."

He reaches out and grabs my hand once more. This time, however, his touch is firm but gentle. My breath catches in my chest. His fingers wrap around my wrist as he slowly raises my hand so that my palm is facing him. The diamond glints back at me, large and dazzling and mocking.

"Hate to break it to you," he says, his voice low yet no less powerful as it ripples over my skin, "but this ring says otherwise."

CHAPTER SEVEN

Gavriil
Four weeks later

PEOPLE MOVE ACROSS the lawn, Chanel dresses and Louis Vuitton suits sparkling under the twinkling lights strung up in the trees. The setting sun casts a rosy glow on the crowd made up of movie stars, platinum-award singers, bestselling authors, fellow billionaires and politicians. Waiters dressed in black tuxedos move through the crowd with silver trays, offering crystal flutes of champagne and some rare oyster only found in a river in France.

I tasked Juliette with creating the wedding of the century. She delivered.

Four weeks ago, I slid my ring onto her finger. She showed up at the Seaside Inn the following morning, agreed to a wedding one month later and vanished just as quickly as she'd arrived. I heard nothing else from her the rest of the day.

I got the first bill the following day. Sarabeth DeLancey, the premier wedding planner in the country, orchestrated the weddings of A-list actors, platinum-selling singers and the children of presidents. She would also be coordinating ours. Sarabeth was the first in a long line of bills that had crossed my desk in the past month.

But Juliette's wanton spending seems to have done the trick. The engagement, and the buzz surrounding our luxurious wedding, has been positive. No one has questioned it. The enemies-to-lovers angle has made Juliette and me a regular feature on West Coast news outlets and social media. That we are turning down every interview request has only increased the hype and speculation about our wedding.

It's been a week since I've seen or spoken to her, other than through text messages. She's played her part well at the events we've attended together, including an engagement dinner hosted by some business associates and their spouses. Every time I'd looked over at her during the evening, she'd smiled, laughed, even laid her hand on top of mine. To anyone watching, all they'd seen was a young woman in love. Exactly what I asked of her.

I thought I had some grasp on who she was, some understanding of her character. Yet she's spent my money as if she'd been born to wealth instead of supposedly loathing it for years. To see how easily she slips into the role of lovestruck fiancée, as well as how quickly she sheds it once we're in the privacy of my car or plane, is unnerving. So is realizing the extent that she's using me. As much as I am her.

Which probably makes us perfect for each other, or at least for the next year we're trapped in this arrangement.

When we're alone, she slips into silence and all but ignores me. The first time it happened, it struck me as petty. But as it continued, over and over every time we were alone, I started to slip back into the past, into a tiny, stuffy room and my mother staring at the wall, ignoring her child in favor of reminiscing about her lost lover.

The lover who had given her five thousand euros when she'd told him she was pregnant and then abandoned her.

The more the past overshadowed my present, the terser I got with Juliette, until we were both practically snarling at each other on the few occasions we talked. The only thing that still lingered was that damned sexual heat. Every time Juliette placed her hand on my arm, dressed in gowns that made her understated beauty shine, I wanted to hide her away, to snap at the men leering at her that she was taken.

Nights have been the hardest. I wake up with a throbbing need pounding its way through my body and phantom moans rippling in my head. I've kept it under control so far. Easy to do when she's been spending her nights elsewhere.

But when she's just next door...

I curl my fingers into a fist and let my nails bite into my palm.

Just two more weeks, I remind myself.

After tonight, we'll fly to France for a two-week honeymoon to keep up appearances. I've booked us suites in Paris and on the river cruise to keep us apart as much as possible when we're alone. When we return to the States, the spotlight on our relationship will die down and we'll go our separate ways for the rest of our farce of a marriage.

We just have to make it through the ceremony first. Juliette's played her part well so far, at least in public. But I won't feel completely settled until she's said *I do* and the countdown to my owning Drakos North America free and clear has officially begun.

I watch as the guests below start to drift toward the beach and the rows of ivory chairs lined up on either side of the aisle. I heard nothing but compliments as guests were welcomed into the foyer of my mansion and escorted into the backyard for preceremony cocktails. There've been no whispers about the will, no speculation about this being an arrangement. The only ugly stories I've seen are the ones theorizing that Juliette is marrying me for my money.

Which, I remind myself grimly, she is. My money and a house.

Unfair for me to feel angry about that. I made the offer of the house. But her asking for money took the image I had of her as a feisty but independent reporter and dismantled it until all I was left of was a woman who, sadly, was just like everyone else.

I had one moment on the flight home from Rêve Beach when I wondered if I was judging too harshly. My mother's absence, both in life and death, had left a gaping hole. As a child, I had hoped the hole might be filled with family, namely my father and brother. When both of those failed, the hole widened until I felt like an empty shell.

A shell that only started to feel complete when I made my first million. When I experienced satisfaction at realizing what I had accomplished on my own. Pride at finally being recognized for what I had achieved. I didn't need love or family. In my experience, those things were fleeting, unreliable.

Juliette had experienced the same loss, the same struggles over the years. She had reached out and grabbed an opportunity with both hands, just as I had.

Yet as I watched her go through the same motions, it seemed…hollow.

Then the bills for the wedding started to roll in. The

overblown spending turned my discomfort to antipathy. Yes, I told her to spend. I have the money. I indulge.

But even this is excessive for me.

I glance at the arch at the end of the orchid-lined aisle, draped in gauzy white fabric and wrapped with the same lights strung up in the trees. The only bill that didn't cross my desk was for her wedding dress. A designer probably donated a gown for the chance to be seen at what one news outlet dubbed the most anticipated wedding of the decade.

I move away from the window and walk to the mirror on the far side of my room. The tuxedo, a dark navy with a black satin collar and matching bow tie, are hand-stitched and fit perfectly. Everything is going according to plan.

So why, I wonder as I stalk back over to the window and shove my hands into my pockets, *am I still unsatisfied?*

The door opens behind me.

"Guests are being directed to their seats."

Rafael joins me at the window in a matching tux with a slim tie. My eyes are drawn to a bear of a man stuffed into a suit moving along the edges of the crowd. Anger stirs, but I squelch it. I'm not wasting emotions on him.

"Michail came."

Rafe leans forward and watches him. "I thought he declined."

"He did."

I watch as he approaches Alessandra. The smile disappears from her face when she sees him. Those two have a history. I'm not sure what it involves, although I can make plenty of guesses as I watch her say something that turns his frown into a glower before she whirls around in a swirl of emerald silk and stalks off.

"I'm surprised you invited him."

I shrug. I don't like him. I don't like what he represents. I despise that our father cared more about telling me about the son he barely knew instead of trying to mend the fractures between us.

But the world now knew about Michail Sullivan Drakos, private security millionaire in his own right and secret son of Lucifer Drakos, thanks to a belated press release arranged by Lucifer before he died. The old bastard just had to have the last word. Leaving Michail off the guest list would have looked petty at best and undermined my image.

A mercenary approach. But I don't make decisions based on emotions.

"Are you sure you want to do this?" Rafe asks quietly.

I smirk. "If you really wanted an answer to that, you would have asked it four weeks ago when I asked you to be my best man."

Silence reigns between us.

"I don't always know what to say."

I glance at Rafael in surprise. My brother is a block of ice. I've never once heard him admit to anything that could resemble a weakness.

"You always know what to say."

"For business, yes." He leans forward, his eyes sweeping across the lawn. "When it comes to personal matters, I'm more of a failure than our father."

I frown. "Are you drunk?"

He laughs, the sound rusty as if he hasn't used his voice for that function in a very long time.

"Sadly, no. Merely reflective."

He looks at me then with that sharp gaze I know so well. Except right now it's tinged with a brotherly concern I've never experienced. It cuts me, unexpected and sharp. When I found out I had a brother, a stubborn flame of hope had flickered to life. Despite my mother choosing heartache over life, and my father dismissing me as if I were nothing more than a bug he'd stepped on, the concept of a sibling—a *brother*—had made me hope one last time.

A hope that died the moment Rafe had walked in on a break from university, said hello as if he was greeting a stranger on the street, and then continued on to his private rooms on the second floor where he stayed until he went back to London a week later.

He was never cruel or rude. His indifference was almost worse.

But I grew up. I shoved all of those hopes and desires for something more, for a family, out of my mind as I hardened my heart.

That a single glance and a few words can shake my resolve makes me feel…weak. Weak and angry that he would choose now, after all these years, to try and be a brother.

"I have concerns about how quickly you rushed into this. And who you're rushing into it with."

"That's the beauty of this arrangement, Rafe." I slap him on the back. "She's agreed to cease any investigations into our company. After we're divorced, even if she does try to write anything, it will look like pettiness from an ex-wife."

"But we don't have anything for her to write about." That look of concern intensifies. It's almost unnatural on a face that's usually as smooth as stone. "We never have, and never will, be like him."

The way he says it with such conviction digs deeper

into my heart. I pause, waiting a second for my emotions to settle before I speak. It's nice to hear, sure.

But it's too late. I'm not opening my heart to anyone again.

"Doesn't mean she won't try to drum up something to get back at Lucifer."

Rafe's brows draw together. "I've wondered why she focused on him so hard. I should look into her background."

I nearly tell him then, about Grey House and her father. At the last second, I bite it back. No matter what I think of her, it's not my story to tell. That's what I tell myself as I ignore the protective instinct that rises.

I glance back out the window, then smile as I see a familiar blond-haired woman moving through the crowd, shoulders thrown back with confidence as she navigates with the use of her forearm crutches.

"Tessa's here."

I can practically hear Rafe's neck snap as his head whips around and he moves to the window. Interesting. I think this is the most emotion I've ever seen him display. His eyes zero in on the petite figure dressed in blue. His wife.

"You invited her?"

"She's family."

There. An almost imperceptible flinch before he regains control.

"Yes. Of course."

He doesn't offer up anything else so I steer the conversation back to my own nuptials.

"Don't worry about Juliette. She's signed the contract." The majority of guests have moved to the beach and are taking their seats. The sun is just about to graze the horizon. In a matter of minutes, I'll be a married man. "Drakos Development is safe."

I can feel Rafe's gaze on me, but I don't look. I've had enough surprises for one evening.

"Business isn't everything, *adelfós*. I hope you learn that before you lose something important."

"I have something important." I look at him then and arch a brow. "My share of the company. I would do anything for it. Including marrying to ensure its legacy." I make a show of glancing down at my watch. "Speaking of, it's time. Shall we?"

I don't bother waiting for an answer. I stride toward the door. A moment later, I hear his footsteps behind me.

As we walk downstairs, Sarabeth materializes at the bottom. With her black hair pulled into an elegant twist on top of her head and a violet-colored sheath dress, she could pass for a guest if she wasn't sporting a headset and a tablet.

"Mr. Drakos, please proceed to the ceremony site. We'll begin the processional in ninety seconds."

I salute her as I pass. The woman would have made a phenomenal drill sergeant.

The quartet reserved for the cocktail hour and ceremony are playing a lighthearted tune as Rafe and I walk down the elevated aisle. I nod to guests and smile, aware of the photographer catching my every move. The photos, and our only interview, have already been sold to a national magazine. An additional investment in making sure the right story is told about our relationship while reaping extra publicity for Drakos North America.

Rafe and I stop before the arch and face the crowd. A flower girl in a blush-colored dress prances down the aisle, scattering scarlet rose petals with an abandon that makes me grin. Catherine, the mother of the little girl and a good friend of Juliette's, follows in a bridesmaid gown the same shade of seductive red that makes her dark brown skin glow. She smiles for the cameras, but I don't miss the sharp glance she serves me as she takes her place on the opposite side of the arch. I only met her for the first time last night at the rehearsal, and Catherine has suspicions.

Smart woman. Fortunately, in the one conversation I had with Catherine, it doesn't appear Juliette has broken her promise. Yet. But Catherine, who has known Juliette for years and has some connection to Juliette's family, isn't buying the whole suddenly-in-love angle. As long as Juliette adheres to the contract, Catherine can cast me all the suspicious looks she wants.

A moment later, the traditional wedding march begins to play as the officiant gestures for everyone to stand.

And then I see her.

The world fades away. My vision becomes a tunnel, my focus solely on the stunning woman at the opposite end of the aisle. Long sleeves made of lace offer tantalizing glimpses of her skin. The low cut of the bodice leaves her shoulders bare and follows the lines of her waist before cascading into a full skirt that makes it seem like she's gliding down the aisle towards me.

The subtle, sexy touches blend with elegance and her natural beauty. Gone is the severe bun or the efficient braid. Her hair flows, dark and wavy, down her back, just like it did that day on the bluff. A veil trimmed in the same lace as her sleeves flutters behind her like butterfly wings. Blush highlights her cheekbones. Her lips, painted a vivid red, are tilted up into the barest of smiles as she nods to some of the guests.

I blink in surprise when I see the woman by her side, moving down the aisle in her wheelchair with one hand on the control and the other wrapped tightly around Juliette's. She'd mentioned someone special was walking her down the aisle but that they had been indisposed for last night's rehearsal.

The woman looks at me, and recognition slams into me. Desdemona Harris. Simon's ex-girlfriend. Silver streaks through her blond hair. The slight wrinkles by her eyes make her appear kind. Her gaze, chocolate brown, is warm but nervous, as if she's not sure what to make of all this. She turns her gaze to Juliette, who looks down at her and smiles with such reassuring warmth it makes me lose my breath.

The tension in their grip pulls me back from my fantasy. Juliette looks back up. Our eyes meet and I see nerves, apprehension.

Beautiful.

I nearly mouth the word to her, to ease the tension in her gaze and build a bridge between us.

But then she shifts, her chin rising as her eyes harden and she stares at me with something akin to disgust even as she smiles so sweetly it makes me want to growl. In that moment I regret the horde watching our every move, the cameras clicking away. I want it to just be the two of us so we can finally rip the gloves off and shout at each other. Something raw and honest, not this brittle chasm that widens with every encounter.

An alarm sounds deep within my mind. I freeze. I can't remember the last time I wanted something messy, craved reality instead of the precise existence I'd crafted for myself. The woman walking toward me, the one I'm about to pledge my life to for the next twelve months, has made me want…more.

I don't want more. I want what I've forged for myself, with no one but me at the helm.

I slip back into the familiarity of my role and shoot Juliette a confident smile as I rake my eyes up and down her body. A different heat is kindled as my gaze lingers on the swells of her breasts above the bodice of her dress, the flare of her hips beneath the gown. A heat made all the more pleasing by the warning look she shoots me as she draws near.

My smile grows. We agreed on no sex. But no one said anything about not looking.

Juliette passes her bouquet to Desdemona and then joins me in front of the officiant. My chest tightens as I wrap her hands in mine, my thumb brushing against her ring. She blinks rapidly as I trace a lazy circle on her skin before tensing in my grasp as I gently press down. I try, and fail, to hide my slight smile as her mask slips and I see the raw need in her eyes.

"Repeat after me, Gavriil."

I repeat the vows spoken by the officiant. No one else seems to notice the slightest hesitation before she repeats her own.

"You may kiss the bride."

I smile at her as my hands settle at her waist and pull her close. My fingertips brush bare skin. Blood surges as my body hardens at the realization that her back is naked.

I lower my head and seal my lips to hers.

Too much. The thought flashes in my mind, then disappears, smothered by the craving ripping through my body.

It's too much for a first kiss. The first kiss between man and wife. The first kiss ever between two people.

But it's happening. It's happening and, *Theós*, I can't stop.

Her taste fills me. Fire licks up my hands, my arms, then flashes down my spine as I press my lips more firmly against hers, tease the seam of her lips with my tongue. Not just to tease, no, but to claim. Even if this is a charade of a marriage, I want everyone to know this woman is *mine*.

I should let go, should be done with it, need to stay in control—

Her lips part. I feel her inhale right before she kisses me back, our parted lips deepening the intimacy between us for a mere second before she suddenly pulls back. I stare at her, my gaze fixed on her face. Her eyes are dark, her breathing heavy. She felt it just as much as I did. That pulsing need, more than desire or mere lust.

What have I done?

Over the roaring of blood in my ears, I hear the cheering of the crowd, the whoops and congratulations.

"I now pronounce you man and wife," the officiant proudly declares.

I recover first and tug her around to face the guests. Their smiles blend together as my mind tries to process what just happened.

I married Juliette Grey. I married her and then I kissed her and now my world feels like it's been tilted off its axis.

I inhale once, exhale slowly. Then I slip an arm around her waist and pull her against my side. She stiffens but doesn't turn away. A quick glance out of the corner of my eye confirms that she's at least trying to smile. But the

stretching of her lips looks more like the grimace of someone about to face a firing squad.

I lean down, my lips brushing her ear and sending a
shiver through her.

"Smile, Mrs. Drakos."

CHAPTER EIGHT

Juliette

I LEAN AGAINST the marble banister, a glass of champagne in my hand and a glimpse of stars above me. The lights of the Queen's Necklace, a collection of opulent homes and buildings on Malibu Bay, glow against the darkening navy of a summer night. Even though I prefer my mist-covered Olympic Coast, it is beautiful.

I smile at the dark waves of the Pacific rolling lazily up onto the beach. Given the sheer size of the ocean, it's odd how it can still feel like a comfort, a familiar friend amidst so many strangers milling just a few dozen feet away.

My moment of peace drifts away as someone laughs behind me. Just one hour ago, I said "I do." Now my gargantuan ring has a mate, a silver monstrosity that has even more diamonds shoved into the band. Its sole purpose is to draw attention to the wealth that purchased it.

Which about sums up my husband in a nutshell.

When Gavriil told me his reasons for wanting an outrageous wedding, I was furious. The man wanted to humiliate me, to put me on display not just for that stupid will, but to show me who had the upper hand in this arrangement.

That he would also be showing the world, again, how much money he had was just a bonus.

Two can play at that game.

I take a drink of my champagne. The bubbles dance on my tongue, leaving behind a taste of citrus blended with honeysuckle. The best champagne I've ever had. Given what it cost, it should be. I wondered if it would be one those luxury items everyone raves about because it's so rare when it's actually terrible.

I'd never heard of king protea flowers or phalaenopsis orchids before I let Gavriil slide that monstrous engagement ring onto my finger. But I made it my mission to do exactly what he said: spend and let the whole world know just how much money he had. But I did it in such a way that even he would be irritated at the amount of money spent.

Judging by the irritation furrowing his brow when I'd handed him the final bill for the catering, I'd accomplished my mission.

He could afford it. I'm comforting myself with knowing Sarabeth worked with Dessie to identify local care centers that would wake up to lavish flowers, carefully packaged Belon River oysters from France, and leftover triple-chocolate cake with raspberry sauce and buttercream frosting. It takes some of the sting out of having just spent over three million dollars on an event that won't last more than eight hours.

A sigh escapes. The question drifts through my mind again—will this marriage, this farce, be worth the price— even though I know it's too late as I avoid looking at the rings.

I also know the answer. All I have to do is look at Dessie to know it was the right choice. Ever since I told her that

Grey House would be mine again, and that I wanted her to move back in with me, she's been on cloud nine. Catherine, whose daughter Whitney served as the flower girl, told me Dessie's been putting more effort into her physical therapy appointments and getting out of her room again.

Those reports came in between concerned questions from Catherine about my engagement and upcoming wedding. Aside from Dessie, she's the only other person who knows why I loathed Lucifer Drakos with every fiber of my being. She's not convinced about this sudden whirlwind romance with Lucifer's son.

But even if I hadn't signed the contract, I would have kept my word. No matter how much I wanted someone to talk to about this crazy scheme I'd landed myself in.

A scheme made all the more ridiculous by my insane attraction to a man I can barely stand. My cheeks heat as I relive that fateful kiss, from the burn of his fingers against my back to that intimate, playful swipe of his tongue against my lips.

Another gulp of champagne fails to cool me off. Not when I'm thinking about how I kissed him back. Just for one second, but the damage was done. That moment when our breaths mingled, when the world around us stilled and we were the only two people caught in the eye of a storm that had been swirling ever since we'd known each other's names.

What am I going to do? I had envisioned the attraction between us as simple, a little more intense than the couple previous relationships I've had, but nothing I couldn't handle.

Except I can still feel his hands on my waist. Can still feel that moment his body went hard and still when I returned his kiss, as if I'd surprised him. Can still see his eyes when we pulled apart, wide and shocked like his world had just been rocked as mine had.

Until he'd turned to face the crowd. Any hints of his true feelings were gone beneath that perfect mask as he'd ordered me to smile.

I'd made it down the aisle and to the cocktail hour with what I'd termed as my *elated bride* face intact. I'd eaten one smoked trout croquette, greeted a handful of people who had a look of importance about them as Gavriil rattled off names I barely heard, given Dessie a hug, and then disappeared into the night with my champagne before she or Catherine could see past my charade.

I have no idea where my husband is. Which is better all around. After our mandatory two-week honeymoon, I'll be able to come up with plenty of excuses to keep my distance for the remainder of our contract. My work, overseeing renovations to Grey House, traveling with Dessie once she's feeling up to it. Anything to keep distance between us, to prevent another kiss from happening.

The salty scent of the sea drifts to me on a breeze. I inhale, my breath a shudder as I admit what I will never confess to another living soul: that Gavriil Drakos, a man who stands for everything I've fought against for years, has the power to consume me. He's the kind of man parents warn their daughters to stay away from. The kind who pulls you so high you know you can fly.

Until they let go of your hand and you plummet back to earth. Alone. Broken.

I press my fingers against the cool stone of the banister. I've seen the women left behind by powerful men, the discarded toys that mean nothing once the novelty's worn off. I may have sold my hand in marriage.

But I refuse to sell my soul to the son of the devil.

Awareness prickles the back of my neck. Above the alluring fragrance of orchids and sea salt, I smell amber and smoky wood. A shiver teases its way down my spine as I fight to keep my face toward the waves.

"You disappeared for so long I wondered if I had a runaway bride on my hands."

His voice slides over my skin.

"Just needed a break. Lot of people."

He moves to the banister next to me. I don't look at him, but I can feel him. Feel the heat of his body, feel his sheer presence.

"Our first dance is in eight minutes."

My lips quirk. "Sounds like Sarabeth found you."

"Found me and gave me marching orders. I should hire her."

I can't help but laugh. I feel him tense beside me, then slowly relax as a chuckle escapes him. Warm and casual, a sound that fills my chest before I can guard myself against it.

"That's a beautiful dress."

Now it's my turn to tense as I finally look at him. The one thing that is mine and mine alone in this sham of a wedding is my dress.

The pissed-off side of me argued for going to the splashiest dress boutique in California and plunking down a hefty sum on a designer gown. Except everything I tried on felt... wrong. Constricting. Fake. I was drawn back time and time again to the cedar chest tucked into my closet in my little cottage. The one my father gave to me before I left to move in with Dessie. The one with my mother's initials carved in the lid.

I have only the flimsiest memories of my mom. They're more impressions than images. Cool glass beneath my hand and the warmth of her body at my back while we watched rain splash the windows of Grey House. A laugh, boisterous and full. A soothing voice when I came home from pre-school crying because my best friend played with someone else. But when I pulled out her wedding dress, I felt her. Relived those wonderful, warm memories as her floral scent, mixed with the faint hint of cedar, drifted up from the lace.

"It's my mother's."

His eyes widen slightly before a shutter drops over them.

"A surprising choice, given your other selections for tonight."

I shrug. He doesn't need to know that I had never envisioned wearing it as my own gown. I'd talked about using part of the train as a veil, or perhaps wrapping a strip of lace around my wedding bouquet to honor my mother. But when I'd pulled it out of the chest, felt that warmth wash over me, I knew I would need that connection today, that remembrance of love, as I walked down the aisle and into a loveless marriage.

"Haven't you heard? Vintage is in."

His eyes narrow, as if he's trying to decipher some puzzle. I'm about to open my mouth and tell him not to bother when Sarabeth materializes out of the darkness.

"There you are!" She taps a finger on the clipboard. "You should have been lined up two minutes ago. Let's go."

Gavriil's lips tilt up. Amusement lights his pale blue eyes as he inclines his head to Sarabeth before extending a hand to me. I ignore him and toss back the rest of the champagne before setting the glass on the banister.

"Charming," he murmurs under his breath as he grabs my elbow and pushes me toward the dance floor.

"At a thousand a bottle, I didn't want to waste any."

His grip tightens and I suppress a satisfied smirk as he leads me to the dance floor. If the man is going to parade me around like a monkey in his personal circus, I'm not going to waste an opportunity to get under his skin.

We near the patio, strung with twinkling lights and sur-rounded by stunning pots overflowing with the ridiculously expensive orchids and dramatic roses. Tables draped in black tablecloths and topped with smaller clusters of the same flower arrangements form a C around the dance floor, with the orchestra on an elevated platform at the far end of the patio.

"Ladies and gentlemen, Mr. and Mrs. Gavriil Drakos!"

The crowd cheers as Gavriil leads me onto the dance floor. I think I'm smiling at the sea of faces blurred by the lights and my own nervousness. The fear that they'll see right through me.

"It's a wonder you managed to gain the reputation you did."

My spine snaps into a straight line as I shoot a steel-laced smile his way.

"Oh?"

He pulls me close, one arm tight about my waist, a hand resting on my naked back and the other wrapped around my fingers.

"For someone with your renown, I expected you not to wear your heart on your sleeve." He leans down, his breath tickling my ear. "At least look happy for your first dance with your new husband."

I smile then, a bright, brilliant beam as I stop myself from stomping on his foot.

"Of course, darling," I croon.

He presses me closer, his eyes flaring as he whisks me into a turn. I grit my teeth against the traitorous pleasure that zips through my veins at the feel of his body against mine. Lights streak by as music fills the air. With the way he's looking at me, the masterful way he's waltzing me about the patio, and the gentle brush of lace against my skin, it would be easy to fall into the illusion. To think that the magic of one gilded night could be carried into the next day and beyond.

I focus on a spot over his shoulder. I just need to get through this dance, and then I'll sit down with Dessie or Catherine.

"Everyone's been telling me they haven't attended a better wedding."

His voice breaks through my thoughts, a touch of cold edging his tone.

"You don't sound pleased."

He shrugs before he raises my hand up and spins me into a turn that has my skirt flaring out. The guests applaud and I swear I hear someone swoon. His palm lands once more on my bare back, making me silently curse myself for asking for a "touch of sexiness" from Catherine's seamstress-friend, who did the alterations.

"I didn't say that."

"You didn't have to."

I can feel him watching me for what can't be more than a few seconds but feels like forever.

"You confuse me. You spent thousands on flowers and champagne. But you wear your mother's wedding dress. You work with one of the most lauded event planners in the country, yet invite less than a dozen guests of your own to our wedding. Your father's ex-girlfriend walked you down the aisle." When my head snaps up, he grins down at me. "Dessie spoke very highly of you when I introduced myself during the cocktail hour." He leans down and I swallow hard, vividly remembering the last time his lips were so close to mine. "You're a puzzle, Juliette. One I want to figure out."

"You don't have to figure me out."

I regret the words almost as soon as they're out of my mouth. Something flashes in his eyes, fleeting but no less potent in its pain.

I've hurt him, and for no other reason other than I want to keep distance between us. I open my mouth, grappling for the right words of apology. But before I can speak, he continues.

"True." He shrugs his shoulders. "This is a business arrangement. Not a relationship. You have the house you want. And the money." He says that with the slightest of sneers in his voice as his words slice through me. "And I have what I want."

"Your share of Drakos Development." I say it almost bitterly, as if I expected something more.

"Yes."

"It's so important you would risk marrying your sworn enemy?"

"I would do anything for it."

I glance around us then, at the people watching us dance. Some look starstruck, others calculating, as if they know something's off, can sense the story we've spun is pure fiction.

"And what if someone finds out? About the will and why we got married?"

"If they agree to keep a private family matter private, nothing." His eyes sharpen to chips of pale blue ice. "But if they threaten me, I'll destroy them."

He watches me, his head cocked to the side, as if waiting to see how I'll respond to this display of power. I'd be lying if I said it wasn't intimidating. But in some twisted way, I'm grateful for it. One kiss made me swoon. His frank words, the reminder of why he married me, help cool some of my desire.

If I can just keep playing his words over in my head, a daily mantra to keep me grounded, I can survive the next two weeks in France.

The music starts to wind down. As he takes me into a final turn, he leans down.

"I do, however, propose one adjustment to our contract."

The glint in his eyes puts me on guard. "Oh?"

"Given how well our first kiss went, perhaps we could do both of us a favor and revise the no physical intimacy clause."

My heart stops. I bite down on my lower lip to stop myself from saying the first word that comes to mind. I can imagine it all too easily: hot, sweaty bodies joining together on top of mussed sheets, questing hands and frantic gasps. An inferno that would ignite every nerve as it destroyed reason and left only pure pleasure in its wake.

Applause sounds like a thunderclap and yanks me from my vision. Gavriil smirks down at me, confident of my decision. The sight of it infuriates me that he would assume I could be swayed by one kiss.

Enrages me that I would be tempted by one kiss.

I slide my arms around his neck and rise up on my toes. Fire flares in his eyes as I draw near...

Then shift at the last minute and brush my lips against his cheek as I steel myself to say what needs to be said. To prevent me from compromising my beliefs any further.

"There will be no revisions," I whisper into his ear. "And if you suggest it again, contract or no, I will walk away from this marriage."

His shoulders tense. He draws back, his gaze hard. He grasps my hand and spins me out. My heart leaps into my throat. Have I gone too far?

"My wife, ladies and gentlemen," he announces in a booming voice. I can hear the promise in his words, the threat. He's got his ring on my finger. He's not letting me go anytime soon. And as much as I want to fight him, to shout out the truth and be done with it, I can't. Not when Dessie is sitting on the fringes next to Catherine with color in her cheeks and hope in her eyes.

His fingers tighten on mine a fraction. I incline my head toward our guests as my body grows heavy.

This is going to be a very long year.

CHAPTER NINE

Gavriil

THE EIFFEL TOWER juts up into the summer sky, proud and dark against a light blue. Some might call it cliché or boring. But for me, the Eiffel Tower is a symbol of longevity, of history and pride.

Yet despite my appreciation for the historic landmark, I've barely glanced at it more than half a dozen times in the three days I've been in Paris. Juliette and I spent our wedding night in the King Suite at The Royal. The bellhop had scarcely closed the door before Juliette cleaved off and walked into the guest room, firmly closing the door behind her. I hadn't bothered to follow. Not after her threat on the dance floor. One that still makes my blood boil thinking about how casually she turned and smiled at the crowd as we walked off the dance floor.

I told myself I could simply shut my desire off. Anger simmered on our wedding night and kept the lust away. Business gave me something to focus on for the first leg of our flight from California to New York. We had just passed over the Rocky Mountains when I got the call I have been waiting for. Louis Paul was contemplating my offer for an entire block of New York City real estate just outside of the Financial District.

Juliette dozed off on the leather couch in my private jet shortly after we took off across the Atlantic. I looked up from a finance report to see her hair slipping loose from her bun and framing her serene face. Need had jolted through me, along with that word that had reared its head during the ceremony.

Mine.

If it had been a simple case of the attraction not being reciprocated, the decision would have been easy. But as I've revisited her threat over the past few days, I realized there was something lingering behind her words. Something buried beneath her bravado.

Fear.

She intrigues me. Entices me. The dichotomies of her character, from feisty reporter and bold mercenary to kind-hearted daughter and sentimental dreamer. Learning she had worn her mother's dress, that she had asked her father's former girlfriend to walk her down the aisle, had taken everything I had been thinking about her during our short engagement and turned it on its head. It had also opened the door for the attraction I'd been fighting to surge through.

An attraction she refuses to acknowledge. We're bound together for a year. Why is she dedicated to celibacy when we clearly have something between us worth exploring and enjoying?

But I also know the value of biding my time. Of watching and waiting. The image of impulsivity and brashness I portray is an illusion, one that has served me well time and again while helping me keep my distance. Without that detachment, I wouldn't be nearly as successful.

So we passed most of the flight in silence. A limo whisked us from the airport to the Shangri-La Paris. There was a brief flicker of excitement on Juliette's face when she saw the Eiffel Tower for the first time. But before I could ask her about it, she lapsed back into silence, her gaze distant and focused on anything but me. I let it go.

For now.

I set up my office on the terrace of our penthouse suite, which included views of the Eiffel Tower, the River Seine and the buildings that made up Paris's 16th arrondissement. The first day, I took her to brunch at a glass-roofed restaurant. Yesterday we went on a private tour of the Louvre after closing. Photos of us entering the museum through the contest pyramid in the main courtyard had already made the rounds on various media circuits, my arm around Juliette's waist as she appeared to glance demurely at the ground.

My jaw hardened. Fortunately, I seemed to be the only one who knew she was doing her best to avoid me, even when we were side by side, being shown some of the rarest and most expensive art in the world.

Other than those two outings, we'd kept our own agendas. Juliette flitted in and out of the suite, sometimes with her camera, sometimes with a shopping bag. She never joined me for meals on the terrace. In fact, she rarely came out at all, except at night right before she went to bed. She'd walk out on the far end of the terrace, arms crossed over her chest as if she were keeping something out, and watch the sparkling lights of the Eiffel Tower at night. Then she'd glance my way, nod, and go back to her room.

I've given her more than enough space and kept our excursions to a minimum. It's time for us to be seen together in a more romantic frame, to refocus the spotlight once more on Gavriil Drakos and his enemy-turned-bride.

And to remind her of what could be between us.

A soft creak sounds behind me. Surprised, I turn in time to see Juliette emerge from her room. *Theós*, she's beautiful. Wet hair, slicked back from her forehead, makes her look younger, more vulnerable. She's wearing a short, white robe and moves through the room with an ease that tells me she thinks it's empty. I did leave earlier to meet with a business associate eyeing a housing project next year in the Hamptons. But when I came back, I thought she was out and would stay out the rest of the day.

I watch her for another moment, the casual confidence of her movements, the relaxed ease of her shoulders as she drifts over to the radio and turns it to a jazz station. You'd think that a fluffy bathrobe would deter sexual fantasies. But the sight of her long legs bare beneath the far too short hemline creates visions of those legs wrapped around my waist. I harden faster than I can suck in a breath.

"Good morning."

Her head snaps to the side and her eyes widen momentarily before she smooths out her features and nods to me. Like a queen nodding to her subjects.

I fight to keep my mouth straight and not let her see that I find her confidence so damned sexy.

"Good morning." She tightens the sash of her robe. "I thought you were still out."

We stare at each other for a moment. Her eyes dart from me to the door. I take pity on her and gesture to the table.

"Would you like some coffee?"

She hesitates, then blinks and gives the tiniest nod of her head.

"That sounds nice. Thank you."

I pour her a cup of coffee and watch as she doctors it with a dash of honey, a generous splash of milk, and a spoonful of sugar.

"I was out. Now I'm back." I top off my own cup as I nod toward the cityscape laid out beyond our balcony. "Enjoying the view."

Her head swings in the direction of the Eiffel Tower. The hint of a smile teases her lips as she gazes at the iron lattice, the blur of shapes behind the metal as the more adventurous climb the numerous steps on their way to the top.

"I've been up since sunrise," she finally says softly.

Her words conjure an image of her waking with golden light filtering through the windows, hair mussed as she rises and eyes heavy with sleep. I raise my cup to my lips as I internally vow that before this honeymoon is over, I will be in her bed one morning to wake her up, to rouse her with deep kisses and slow strokes until she's crying out for me.

"Working?" I ask, my voice only a touch gravelly.

She shakes her head. "Sort of. More of a personal hobby I once enjoyed." She shrugs. "Maybe it'll turn into something."

"Oh?"

Her gaze refocuses on me, her eyes narrowed, as if she's trying to determine if I'm genuinely interested or if I have an ulterior motive in mind. I maintain her gaze. Yes, I want her to agree to amend the damned contract. But I'm genuinely curious as to what she'll do next if she truly plans to honor her commitment to not pursue any more stories about Drakos Development.

"Something new. Nothing to do with corporations," she adds with an arched brow.

"I feel safer already."

Her barest huff of a laugh fills me. I don't want to have as strong of a reaction as I do, to be as aware as I am of the little nuances and subtleties of her body language. But I can't help it. I'm not just enjoying the chase. I'm enjoying her company. And she seems to be enjoying mine. Perhaps convincing her to spend the afternoon out where we can be seen and play up the lovesick honeymooners won't be so challenging.

"Can you talk more about it?"

She dips her head. Pink changes her cheeks. It takes me a moment to realize it's not coyness but shyness. She's nervous about whatever the special project is. That hint of vulnerability tugs at me.

"Not yet. It's still in its infant phase."

She looks at me then. Her unexpectedly sweet and self-conscious smile stabs straight into my chest. Her fire, her passion, even her determination, all of it intrigues me. Coupled with this unexpected softness, from the way I saw her check in on Dessie throughout the wedding to the shy excitement adding a sparkle to her eyes right now, is alluring in a way I've never experienced before. I've never been interested in looking past the surface.

Until the woman sitting across from me caught my attention with her daring in standing up to Lucifer. The first person outside my family I'd ever seen risk his wrath.

"Are you moving away from investigative reporting?"

Some of the light dims.

"I don't know. My last job…" Her throat moves as she swallows hard. "It was more challenging than I expected."

I watch her as she raises her coffee to her lips, her gaze distant. I start to ask more, but my phone rings. I glance down. Anticipation zings through me as I recognize the number for Paul Properties offices in New York City.

I glance up. She's looking at me now. I've never hesitated in taking a work call. But after what she's just alluded to, I pause.

"Go ahead." She smiles. "I'm okay."

I move into the living room and take the call from one of Paul's numerous lawyers. The property I want to buy is in a neighborhood that most people have written off. But I had seen the early signs of rejuvenation. The investment in local businesses, the efforts of residents to organize neighborhood watches, community gardens, and other activities that bolstered the rate of people moving in while reducing crime. There are still problems, but there's a lot of potential.

Unlike my early years in the slums of Santorini, I now had both the money and power to turn that potential into something concrete. Something that hasn't become a focus until recently. My only objective when I first started with Drakos Development had been to make as much money as possible. But that goal has evolved, especially in the last year or so as the money hasn't brought as much contentment, as the sensation of wielding power and influence has dulled. My goals now include bettering the communities surrounding my properties. Maybe it will do nothing.

But maybe it will make a difference for someone. Someone like my mother who had someone like me who loved them, despite their numerous faults. Someone who, with the right support, might be able to do what my mother failed to do and climb out of their pit.

I'm not ready to share this new focus with the public. Not yet. Knowing it's rooted in my own painful past is a vulnerability I'm not ready to share. Six minutes later, after answering numerous questions I know were more designed to test me than to divine any information, I hang up and return to the terrace.

Just in time to see my wife with her head tilted to one side as she reads the file I left open on the table.

I freeze, watching as she cranes her neck to read more. Betrayal rips through me so fast I barely contain my snarl. I stalk over, reach down, and snatch the file from under her nose.

"It didn't take you long to break our bargain."

She stares up at me with a wrinkle between her brows and an innocent expression on her beautiful face.

"What are you talking about?"

I dangle the folder from my fingertips.

"Tell me, did you decide to marry me because it might give you access to some of the corporate bigwigs you've been trying to take down? Or was that just a side benefit in addition to the two million dollars?"

Her face pales.

"Do you truly think so little of me? That I wouldn't stand by our contract?"

"The story is the most important thing to you."

She sets her coffee cup down with careful precision, stands and walks to the edge of the terrace. Her shoulders are tense, her chin lifted. But beneath the bravado is a painful sadness that pierces my anger and leaves me feeling like an ass. She looks away from me and out over the rooftops of Paris.

Damn it. I don't know why she was reading the file. But it's not like I walked in on her trying to break into a safe. She glanced at papers I left out on the breakfast table. Instead of asking like a sane person, I jumped to conclusions and lashed out.

I walk up next to her and stop a couple feet away. An apology doesn't seem like enough.

I follow her gaze down to the road below us. A couple walks down the sidewalk, a blond man in a T-shirt and shorts with his arm wrapped about the waist of a red-haired woman. They stop on the corner. The man grabs her close and dips her back, kissing her laughing lips as if he doesn't have a care in the world.

My gaze moves back to her face. She's still watching them, and in that moment I feel more like my father than I ever have before. I'm being cruel, pushing her away because for two minutes we had a conversation that stirred something more than lust or the casual apathy I've coasted on the past twenty-four years, and this made the sense of betrayal that much harsher.

"Perhaps the story is the most important thing."

My gaze sharpens on her face. She continues to watch the couple below.

"But when I care about the story, I care about the people in it, too." She whirls around suddenly, and jabs a finger toward my chest. "I don't care about the payday or what I could buy. I care about justice, about giving a voice to those who have been silenced by people like your father."

Frustration and anger wipe away most of my guilt. Does she think I'm blind? That I didn't pay attention to the numerous bills crossing my desk, to what she's been doing while she's here in Paris?

"You don't care about the payday, but you ask for two million, spend nearly double that on the wedding, and came back yesterday with a bag from Louboutin?"

Instead of dissolving into tears or slapping me across the face, she merely leans back and cocks an eyebrow in my direction, all traces of shyness gone. And damn it if that casual confidence doesn't shoot straight down into my groin and make my blood pulse.

"Coming from the man worth billions and wearing a three-hundred-dollar Hermès tie to drink coffee on a terrace, that insult doesn't carry the sting you want it to."

Frustrated, I rake my fingers through my hair.

"I don't want to insult you, Juliette. I told you before, you confuse me and I reacted—"

"Like a jerk?"

"I was going to say *gáidaros*, but close enough."

She doesn't back down. No, she tosses those shoulders back, the robe partially falling aside and giving me a glimpse of the swells of her breasts. Unlike that tantalizing neckline of her wedding dress, though, there are no layers of lace, no buttons. Nothing but air between me and the woman I'm longing to possess.

The woman I need to touch, now, even if I'm damned for it.

I close the distance between us. She watches me, her body poised to flee. But she doesn't. I reach out. She freezes but doesn't pull away as I glide the back of my hand down the curve of her face.

"What are you doing?" she whispers, her chest rising and falling as a blush twines up her neck.

"Touching you."

She inhales, her eyes burning into mine. "Why?"

"Because you make me hunger." I wrap my arms around her waist and slowly pull her against my chest, savoring the anticipation. "Because no matter how much you confuse me, I can't stop thinking of your lips beneath mine. Of how you felt in my arms." I stop, hovering my lips just above hers. "Tell me to stop, Juliette."

I wait for her to push me away, to remind me of her threat from our wedding day or call me a name and storm off.

But it's Juliette, so she does the last thing I expect. She throws her arms around my neck and kisses me.

CHAPTER TEN

Juliette

I'VE MADE A MISTAKE. I know it as soon as our lips crash together. Mingled harsh breaths, his heartbeat racing beneath my palm as I rest my hands on his chest and press myself against him. I've never done this, never thrown myself at a man because I either had to kiss him or go up in flames.

Our wedding kiss, as unexpected as it was, had the tether of being in front of hundreds of people. It could only go so far. Even our excursions around Paris, as we held hands at the café or he slid a possessive arm around my waist at the Louvre, had been for the benefit of anyone watching.

Here, there's only us. No excuses. And as I respond with an aching need that makes my whole body throb, I have no regrets. Not when his arms are around me like bands of steel, his groan filling me, his hard length pressing against my hips. I'm acutely aware that there's only my robe and the fabric of his pants between the most intimate parts of our bodies.

I slide my hips up and down just a fraction. The friction on my sensitive skin makes me tremble.

"Theós."

He growls it against my mouth as he spins me around

and pulls me into the privacy of the penthouse. Cool air kisses my skin and I glance down to see my robe parted, revealing my breasts. It should make me feel self-conscious, embarrassed.

But when I look up and see Gavriil staring at me like he's starving and I'm the only thing that can satiate his hunger, all I feel is a reckless boldness urging me on.

I step back. Need a moment, just a moment to think. Gavriil's hands tighten momentarily on my waist before he releases me, the tendons in his neck straining as he sucks in a shuddering breath. Seeing his restraint, his respect even as he devours me with ravenous eyes, pushes me through that last moment of hesitation.

I surge forward again, my hands sliding up over his chest as our mouths meet. It's not a kiss but a branding I feel through my chest, through the pulsing in my core, all the way to my toes as his tongue sweeps inside my mouth in an intimate caress that makes me moan.

His hands dive into my hair, anchoring my head as his lips trail over my jaw before he nips my neck. The graze of teeth on sensitive skin makes me cry out and arch against him. I press my hips against his, pressure building as wetness slicks my thighs.

"Gavriil…"

He nudges one leg between mine as he holds me against him. I shift, the friction of his pants against my bare skin making me pant. His mouth descends to the curve of my shoulder, then farther down. One tug and my robe falls open, baring my naked body to his gaze.

"Ómorfi."

The word ripples through me. I don't know any Greek,

but I don't need a dictionary to feel the meaning. To feel beautiful. Seen.

Before I can claw back enough of my sanity, Gavriil dips his head and sucks my nipple into his mouth. Sensation spears out, heated energy whirling through my body as my fingers slide into his hair.

"Gavriil!"

His tongue swirls over me. His hair, thick and silky beneath my hands, is a lifeline as I spiral upward. He keeps one arm banded around my waist as his other hand cups my other breast.

He pulls back. I moan, not wanting this to be it, to live with this unbearable pressure seething beneath my skin, electricity crackling through my veins as if I might combust unless I find some kind of release—

He sweeps me into his arms and stalks over to the couch. I take advantage of my proximity to his neck and repeat what he did to me, kissing his heated skin before I run my tongue over the hollow at the base of his throat.

A growl rumbles in his chest before he sets me down on the couch facing him. He grabs my knees and spreads my legs. I should be embarrassed. I should stop. I should definitely stop.

Not a chance.

His next kiss is fierce, one I return with my need growing to unbearable proportions. I don't know why I'm responding to him with such wild abandon. Maybe it's because I have no vengeance to achieve, to focus on to the detriment of everything else. Maybe this is the distraction I need as I try to figure out the rest of my life.

Or maybe it's simply this man. This man who infuriates and impresses and seduces.

I tense as he glides one hand up my leg, pauses at the top of my thigh and taps out a teasing dance with his fingertips.

"Please, Gavriil."

I don't care that I'm begging, that I'm letting him see just how deeply he affects me. All I care about is being touched, feeling wanted by this man I'm married to.

His hand skims higher. His fingers gently stroke, light touches that tease and stoke the flames higher as he uses his other hand to pull my robe down to my waist and move his mouth down to continue his sensual assault with tongue and teeth on my other breast.

"You're so wet."

I cry out as he slides one finger inside me. It only takes a few long, slow strokes for the peak that's been building since he stalked toward me on the terrace to burst.

"Oh, God!"

It shatters through me, tiny peaks of light spiraling from my core throughout my body. He continues to make love to my breasts with gentle kisses as I drift down from my peak. The soft press of his lips against my skin makes my eyes grow hot. I hadn't imagined such gentleness from him. It shouldn't matter.

Can't matter.

As the pleasure slips away, intrusive thoughts try to break through. Reminders to keep my guard up, to not let this become a habit and risk sliding in deeper. I shove them away as he eases me back to rest against the back of the couch. A lazy smile curves my lips as I recline against silk. For right now, I'm going to focus on feeling. Enjoying.

My eyes fly open as Gavriil pulls my robe back up. I look up to see him watching me. For a moment, there's something in his eyes. Something that kindles a different spark deep inside my chest.

And then it's gone, replaced with his usual languid expression of superiority.

"Should I take this as your agreement to amending the contract?"

I stare at him. Humiliation burns away the lingering tendrils of desire. For one horrible moment, I think I might cry.

No.

He's not worth it. He might not be the lawbreaking bastard I had suspected him of being. But he's still a bastard, incapable of anything but arrogant humor and pompous pride.

I stand, taking vicious pleasure in watching his eyes slide down to the bared skin of my chest. I take my time pulling the lapels of the robe closed and belting it, never taking my eyes off him. I run a hand through my hair and give him a cool smile.

"I don't think what just happened counts as anything meaningful. So, no."

His face tightens. Perhaps in anger or chafed pride. I don't really care. His ego deserves a beating.

"Enjoy your coffee."

I walk to my room and close the door softly behind me, not bothering to lock it. He won't come after me.

I tell myself it doesn't matter. I insist on it even as tears burn the backs of my eyes.

CHAPTER ELEVEN

Juliette

I STAND IN front of the mirror and smooth my hands over the skirt of my dress. I've always paid for good quality clothing. But I've never indulged in luxury before. I never understood why people bothered to spend hundreds or even thousands of dollars on a shirt or dress that would end up with a stain on it the next day.

But right now, standing in front of the oval mirror with the lights of Paris at my back, I understand a little. I was walking down the Champs-Élysées earlier this morning when I passed a boutique store. It was so unlike the other gilded storefronts lining the historic road. The dresses in the window were simple yet elegant.

The dress I'm wearing now, with a Queen Anne neckline that adds a touch of regalness to the simple silhouette, was front and center. Colored a periwinkle blue, with a full skirt falling from the waist and a deep V in the back that bares my skin. Combined with the pearl studs I brought from home and my own hair twisted up into something as close to a chignon as I could get, I feel beautiful.

Beautiful.

The word flickers through me, brings back that moment

this morning when he whispered that word and it pulsed through me like a heartbeat.

My eyes grow hot and I turn away from the mirror. When he kissed me, when he…touched me, I felt alive. Sensual.

The bastard had ruined it all with one of his casual quips. A reminder that what happened between us had been simple pleasure. Yes, he obviously found me attractive. But I have no interest in going to bed with someone who treats sex so casually. I most definitely have no interest in sleeping with someone who doesn't trust me and, I suspect, doesn't even really like me. *A mutual feeling*, I remind myself as I move toward the door. I don't trust him either. How could I when he moves in the world he does, with money ruling his decisions? When he's made it clear his bank balance is the pinnacle of his existence?

My father thought the same thing in the last year of his life. His obsession pushed away the two women who would have loved him to hell and back.

I wasn't trying to be sneaky when I read that file. I'd glanced down as I'd reached for a spoon. The name at the top of the paper had jolted me into action.

Louis Paul. The same man who had been staying at Peter Walter's mansion in an exclusive gated community outside Dallas seven months ago when my investigation led to a raid on the warehouse. A raid that resulted in the rescue of nearly half a dozen human trafficking victims.

Paul came out clean. He'd known Walter for years but had never done business with him. There was no evidence of Paul being involved. Even though I hadn't been actively investigating Paul, I'd kept an eye on him and noted two more trips to Dallas in the past year. Those trips, however, were much more discreet. Paul flew commercial, arrived and left in taxis instead of his usual limo and disappeared into the Dallas suburbs instead of a ritzy hotel downtown.

Yet I couldn't connect him to anything. And then Lucifer had passed away and Paul faded to the back of my mind. Seeing his name on a possible business deal with Drakos North America was jarring. I thought about telling Gavriil when I saw Paul's name on the file. That is, until he stormed in and accused me of using our marriage as an espionage tactic.

Fine. If he doesn't want to bother digging into the backgrounds of people he does business with, then he can suffer the consequences. Just confirms what I suspected all along, too. Gavriil doesn't care who he does business with so long as it gets him what he wants.

My breath rushes out. Even if I'm not confident in my future career, the habits I've developed won't let me back down. That and an irrational desire to not see Gavriil connected to someone who might be a different kind of a monster than his father, but a monster nonetheless. I don't know why I care. Only that I do. Which is why I sent a few texts to my most reliable sources. It's probably nothing, but I've never left things like this up to chance.

And if you do find something? What then?

I don't know if Gavriil would even believe me if I do uncover something. His accusations before our interlude on the couch showed me exactly how little he thinks of me. But he doesn't seem the type to ignore hard evidence, even if he doesn't like the findings. I've also caught glimpses now and then of a different side of him. The tender respect he gave Dessie after I introduced them after the ceremony. His genuine happiness when I saw him chatting with his sister-in-law Tessa during the reception. The man likes to act like he has no soul. From what I've seen, though, he has one. He's just buried it so deep under what I can only suspect is years of hurt and rejection that most people don't see it.

I stalk to the window and lean my forehead against the cool glass. I don't want to see these glimpses. It twists my feelings for him up in knots, complicates what should be a case of simple lust and adds an edge to it. A very dangerous edge that can only lead to heartache.

My phone buzzes and my stomach drops. My fifteen-minute warning before I have to present myself like the dutiful wife and accompany my husband to whatever activity he's planned for us to be seen by the general public.

The brunch had been casual but delicious, a welcome reprieve after being cooped up in a plane for hours on end. The private tour of the Louvre had also been fascinating. I'd kept my face passive throughout, not wanting to do something that would be untoward for the wife of a billionaire and betray that I was a complete and total fraud, like tear up at the sight of the headless winged goddess guarding the top of the Daru staircase or let my mouth drop open at the sight of *the* Mona Lisa.

No, the scheduled activities haven't been excessive. While I've done my best to maintain the bored façade I'm sure most people in my position would assume, I've enjoyed our excursions, even if it irks me to admit it. But it still makes me feel like an experiment under a microscope.

After our encounter this morning, I got dressed and left the penthouse as quickly as possible. It took me a good hour of wandering up and down random streets for my heart to quiet and some of the ache to lessen. I spent the next hour with my camera, taking shots of the winding streets and shops. I snapped a dozen or so portraits, too, mostly of Paris residents, but a couple expatriates and a group of tourists.

The more time I've spent with my camera, drafting passages about the people I've met and the stories they've shared, the more I've felt my heart respond in a way it hasn't in a long time. When I was younger, before Lucifer Drakos came to Grey House, I wanted to be an author. In middle school, I fell in love with photography. Sure, I took some of my own photos for my investigations, but that wasn't the primary focus.

I glance at my camera. It's nearly time to join Gavriil for whatever he has planned for this evening. But I can't resist flipping the camera on and toggling through the photos. An old man with bronzed skin and a face covered in wrinkles sitting outside his coffee shop. A clay mug full of coffee brewed with cinnamon and sugar, steam curling up from the surface. Two kids standing with chocolate ice cream dripping down their hands as they smile in front of the crowds lining up to see the restored Notre-Dame Cathedral.

There are stories here. The everyday people I'd missed so much of in my quest to bring down the criminal elite. The shop owner emigrated from Mexico over forty years ago after he fell in love with a French woman on a trip to see Sinatra sing in Las Vegas. The two kids are here with their mother and grandparents after losing their father in a car accident. It's the first time, their mother confided in me with tears in her eyes, that she's seen them happy in nearly a year.

A part of me still clings to the possibility of jumping back into my investigative work. It doesn't seem possible that something that has been such a huge part of my life, all the way back to my last years of high school when I started working for the school newspaper and applying for scholarship after scholarship, is over.

But as I turn the camera over in my hands, anticipation flickers through me. Not the demanding urgency of my investigative reporting. Not the thrill of elation when I knew I'd caught someone, a thrill that had turned into something ugly. My version of wealth was the knowledge I hoarded and the power I used to bring them down.

My fingers lightly trace the dials and buttons on top of the camera. This excitement is different. Innocent, new. Something wholly mine. Even if there are fewer jobs and less pay in the areas of photography and photojournalism, I don't want this next chapter of my life to be rooted in money. I want it to be founded on something more than death and revenge.

I switch off the camera and tuck it back into its case. I still have time. Almost a whole year. Even after the renovations I'll be making to Grey House, I'll have a tidy sum left over that, with the right investments, can keep Dessie and me going while I try to figure the rest of my life out.

I walk toward my closet where I have some sensible flats tucked away. My eyes stray to the gold shopping bag, the red tissue paper peeping over the edge. I pause. The trip into the Louboutin store was a spur-of-the-moment decision following a text from Catherine that Dessie had started a new round of physical therapy and had already shown marked improvement. Her relapse appeared to be subsiding this time. I bought her a pair of blush-colored ballet flats with cute straps that wrapped around the heel and the signature red outsole.

And yes, I think with no small amount of acrimony, I bought a pair of heels for myself. A dress and shoes. Anyone would have thought I'd spent another three million dollars by the way Gavriil had snapped at me earlier.

The man really is a pompous jerk. The thought propels me across the room to the bag. I bought them with my money. Would I have bought them without two million sitting in a high-interest savings account? No.

But I bought them for me using money I had before I agreed to this ridiculous arrangement, and I'm going to wear them because I want to. If he doesn't like it, I can just slip off a shoe and jab him with it.

A highly improbable scenario. I'm not going to jail over him. But it brings a smile to my face nonetheless as I set the bag on the bed and reach inside.

I pull out the heels, nude leather with the sole and stiletto heel colored red. Thankfully the store offered a variety of heel heights. The assistant who helped me, an older man with a thick silver beard and a kind smile, had helped me try on several before I found one I semitrusted myself not to tip over in.

I slip the heels on and stand. I glance at the mirror again. I've always believed vanity to be one of the worst sins, especially with how much I've seen it in the people I've investigated over the years.

But as I look at my reflection, I don't try to stop the rush of pleasure and confidence. I look good. No, I look great.

With a smile on my face, I open my door and nearly walk straight into my husband.

"Good eve…"

His voice trails off as he rakes me from head to toe with a searing gaze. I clutch my handbag with both hands, willing myself not to feel anything at his blatantly appreciative appraisal.

"Ready?"

"Yes." I strive for an indifferent tone, as if he hadn't just had his mouth on my breasts a few hours ago. "Where are we going?"

"It's a surprise. The limo's waiting downstairs."

I give him the ghost of a smile. He holds out his arm and I slide my hand into the crook of his elbow as he escorts me out of the suite. I force the smile into something a little more lovesick when the elevator doors open to the lobby. Most people glance at us and look away. A few, though, stare. One pulls out their phone and snaps a photo.

My breath rushes out once we're in the limo, the tinted windows giving me at least a few minutes' peace. Gavriil takes the seat opposite me. He leans back into the leather and drapes one arm across the top as he stares at me, his gaze assessing.

"Relax, Grey. It's not a bad thing to be seen with your husband."

I shrug. "For all intents and purposes, Drakos, you're not my husband. We're business acquaintances. I know these… field trips have a purpose. I'm just not used to the scrutiny."

I say the words, even if my heart twists inside my chest at the lie. Feeling like a bug under a magnifying glass is draining. But so is trying to keep my walls up. Especially after what happened between us earlier. I need to back away. Maintain the distance I'd established during our wedding and kept up until this morning.

"Many people would enjoy this."

"I'm not most people."

"No, you're not." Something that looks astonishingly like regret crosses his face. "I have no excuse for earlier.

What I said was crass and rude, both before and after we kissed. Let me make it up to you."

I almost ask why. Why did he say something so horrid?

But asking for a reason, giving him a chance to explain, could take me back to that line I'd straddled this morning. Reintroduce the traces of emotional intimacy that had developed during our coffee on the terrace.

It's not worth the risk. So I simply nod, telling myself I can stay strong even as my heart whispers a warning.

CHAPTER TWELVE

Juliette

TEN MINUTES LATER, my jaw drops open as the limo crosses the arches of the Pont d'Iéna. The Eiffel Tower literally sparkles against the backdrop of a rose-streaked night sky as the limo pulls up to the curb.

"I saw it the other nights, but up close…" My voice trails off as my heart surges in my chest. "I wanted to come here before we left."

The limo driver opens the door and we step out onto a sidewalk teeming with people. Some are posing for photos with the Tower behind them. Others are kissing or simply ogling the sight of one of the most iconic structures in the world. Between the massive iron legs holding its incredible weight aloft, I can see the green park on the other side dotted with picnickers.

"Is the restaurant off the Champ-de-Mars?" I ask as Gavriil puts a guiding hand to my back.

"Not quite."

We walk through the crowds to the south pillar. A short set of stairs leads inside.

"Inside the Tower?"

My voice sounds breathless, but I don't care. I've heard

of the restaurant, seen the reviews, the mouthwatering photos of gourmet cuisine on Instagram.

"Yes."

He sounds amused, but when I glance up at him, he's smiling down at me like he's pleased with my excitement. I brush aside any self-consciousness as I commit to enjoying the evening ahead of me.

An elevator whisks us up to the restaurant, located on the second floor of the Tower. Our table is right by the window. Boats drift down the Seine. The wings of the Palais de Chaillot on the other side of the river are lit up with golden light. In the distance, I can see the dome of the Basilique du Sacré-Cœur de Montmartre.

A waiter in a dark suit approaches our table and greets us in French as he hands us menus.

"*Bonjour* and good evening," Gavriil replies.

"Good evening and welcome. May I start you off with a glass of wine?"

"*Un verre de rosé, s'il vous plait.*"

I smile as Gavriil looks at me in surprise before ordering himself a glass of merlot, in French as well.

"Dessie insisted I take a foreign language in high school," I say in response to his unasked question after the waiter takes our orders for the seven-course tasting. His brows draw together. "I fell in love with French and kept it up in college."

My phone vibrates in my handbag.

"I'm sorry, do you mind if I check that?"

At his nod, I pull my phone out. Alarm skitters through me.

"It's Catherine."

"Go," he says as he stands, waiting for me to leave before he sits back down.

I walk away from the dining area as I answer.

"Catherine? What's wrong?"

"Nothing's wrong." My friend's voice is practically vibrating with excitement. "I'm sorry, you're probably out to dinner or something naughty—"

"Cate!" I break in with a laugh as my heart rate steadies. "What's going on?"

"She's walking again."

My vision swims as tears fill my eyes. I blink them back and take in a deep, shuddering breath as relief swamps me.

"Thank God."

"That's all. She asked me to call, she was exhausted after physical therapy and went to sleep almost as soon as we got her back to her room. But she's better, Juliette. She's getting better every day."

We say goodbye. I linger in the vestibule for a moment. Dessie's getting better. We'll have a follow-up with her doctor when I get back and learn more about what the future may hold. But right now, in this moment, Dessie's walking. I'm in Paris dining in one of the most incredible restaurants in the world. And, shockingly, I'm enjoying Gavriil Drakos's company.

That's enough right now.

I'm not going to question it. I'm simply going to enjoy the evening.

I return to the table. Our wines have been delivered. Gavriil is looking out the window, one hand resting on the stem of his glass, his handsome profile in stark relief against the encroaching night.

My breath catches.

Focus on the moment. Just tonight. Nothing else.

"Everything all right?" he asks as I sit.

I nod. "Just an update on Dessie's physical therapy."

The waiter delivers the first course: beets folded over blue cheese and Greek yogurt, sprinkled with cilantro and pumpkin seeds, and served with toasted crackers.

I take my first bite and barely bite back a moan.

"Is this how you eat all the time?" I ask as I force myself to go slow and savor every bite.

"Believe it or not, I like burgers, too," he replies with a grin. "You said Dessie insisted you take a foreign language. Did you live with her after you disappeared from Rêve Beach?"

Thankfully, I had just slid a cracker into my mouth, giving me a moment to think about how much detail I want to share. He already knows so much about me.

On paper, I think as my chest tightens at how he looked down at me with disgust right before touching me so intimately.

Good enough for a quick fling, but not good enough to spend his money or trusted to keep my end of our bargain.

Stop. I'm not going to let anyone else ruin my evening. He's playing nice right now. I can do the same.

"When things with my dad went downhill, I moved in with Dessie in Seattle."

His lips flatten into a line. "I'm sorry."

I shrug and focus on my food. "It was a long time ago."

"Doesn't mean it doesn't still hurt."

I stab a beet with my fork. This isn't the conversation I want to be having. I want to enjoy my meal, the sight of Paris at twilight, the knowledge that Dessie is doing better.

I look up to tell him just that...

…then falter at the faint glimmer of pain in his eyes. A pain I know all too well.

"Who did you lose?"

He blinks. For a moment I think he's going to make a joke or dismiss the question.

"My mother."

I've never heard so much conveyed in just two words. Grief, loss, anger, regret. Emotions that take my assumptions about Gavriil Drakos's childhood and turn them on their head.

"I'm…" My voice trails off and I swallow hard. "You're right. There are weeks and even months where everything seems fine. And then you see something or smell something or hear something and it takes you right back."

"What takes you back?"

Don't.

My heart shouts at me to stop, to keep myself intact. But he's looking at me now with a different kind of hunger lurking behind his mask. A need to connect with someone who understands. I know deep in my bones this is not something he has revealed to many, if anyone.

"Popcorn." My eyes burn and I look back down, stirring crumbles of blue cheese around my plate. "When I was little, I would get scared of the storms. I thought the rain and lightning would drag Grey House into the sea." I pause, giving myself a moment to let the wave of anger and anguish crest, subside. "So Dad would make popcorn. We'd sit in my window seat and watch the storm until it passed like it was a movie."

His eyes burn into mine. "My father took that from you."

My throat tightens. "He did. But my father didn't do

himself any favors. His obsession with making it big started him down that road in the first place."

Gavriil's lips part slightly as understanding dawns. That it's not just his father who created my fixation, but the actions of my own, the greed that drove him away from his daughter and the woman who loved him.

Needing to get back on firm ground, I ask, "What takes you back?"

He blinks and looks out over the city. He stares so long at the lights flickering on as night drifts in I wonder if he's going to answer.

"Scratching."

I frown. "Scratching?"

"In the walls. On the floor at night." The twist of his lips is quick, harsh as he glances at me. "Rats."

The horror of his answer has me reaching for him before I can stop myself. I nearly lay my hand over his when the waiter arrives with our second course. I snatch my fingers back just in time. But it doesn't stop the physical ache inside me, the hurt for what he must have endured in those lost years before arriving at Lucifer's villa.

The waiter sets bowls of squash soup topped with green onions and a swirl of coconut milk in front of us. China clinks in the background. Someone laughs. Soft, seductive jazz plays from hidden speakers. Gavriil recovers first, picking up his spoon as he shoots me a casual smile, as if apologizing for sharing something so terrible. I start to reassure him, but he speaks first.

"Tell me more about Dessie."

Right now I'd tell him almost anything. Anything to take his mind away from the hell of his past.

"Like what?"

"Like why your father's ex-girlfriend accompanied you down the aisle."

"She's a second mother to me. The one constant I've had in my life. I wouldn't be who I am today without her."

"She loves you."

There's a tinge of envy to his voice, an underlying heartache that further cracks the vision I've carried of Gavriil for so long—impervious, cavalier, uncaring.

"She does. She gave me a home when I needed it the most. And now I can give her one."

The jolt is so small I nearly miss it, a flash of tension through his body as his eyes widen.

"Everything okay?"

"Yes." A slight shake of his head. "I haven't revisited my past in a long time. It threw me off."

The first things that come to mind all sound trite, bland words that don't come close to addressing the bits and pieces he's revealed.

"I can't imagine," I finally say softly.

"Most can't."

The salad arrives. I glance down, registering the artful arrangement of asparagus, mushrooms and artichokes on top of a bed of greens glistening with vinaigrette and flecked with Parmesan. How can I eat like this, be surrounded by this kind of luxury, when the man across from me has just shared something I can't even begin to comprehend?

Gavriil was eight when he went to live with Lucifer. Which means what should have been some of the happiest years of his childhood were spent in hell. A hell that, judging by Gavriil's borderline hatred of his father, Lucifer continued in his own twisted way.

"Money can corrupt."

My head snaps up. Gavriil is watching me, his expression languid except for the sharpness in his gaze. His fingers trail up and down the stem of his wineglass.

"It can." I release a pent-up breath as I reconcile this glimpse into Gavriil's childhood with his obsession with wealth. "It can also be used for good."

He nods, his shoulders relaxing a fraction. "Agreed. Or it can be the one thing that gives back. The only thing."

My heart cracks.

"What about your brothers?"

His chuckle is a dark, sinister sound that nevertheless rolls through me, stirring the embers left from the morning when I bared myself to him.

"I met Michail at Lucifer's will-reading. The same day I learned my father had tied all of my hard work to his own obsessive need to control everything, even in death. And Rafe has always preferred his own company."

If Rafael Drakos was in front of me right now, I would toss my very expensive wine in his face. He's ten years older than Gavriil, which means he would have been eighteen when Gavriil went to live with Lucifer. More than old enough to take a little brother who'd just lost his mother under his wing. To protect him and give him at least a taste of family.

"Just as bad as Lucifer."

Gavriil slowly shakes his head. "Unfortunately, no. It would be so much easier to hate him if he was. But Rafe is just…cold. Straight down to his icy heart. As much as I sometimes want to punch him, I can only imagine what turned him into what he is."

He shakes his head then and signals for the waiter. He

orders us each a glass of pinot noir before changing the topic to what my favorite exhibit was at the Louvre, then skillfully guiding the conversation to the traveling I did for my job. He does it so well I almost forget the rips in our souls we've bared to each other as we eat our way through rosemary risotto topped with beef fillet and shaved truffles. When Gavriil feeds me a bite of chocolate ganache topped with a roasted strawberry, I see the heat in his eyes as my lips part for him.

My body responds to his desire without hesitation. Things have changed between us. The intimacy of sharing so many secrets, of feeling his support and compassion, has built a bridge between us.

I'm now terrified I won't be able to stop myself from crossing it. Even if it means I leave this marriage divorced and brokenhearted.

CHAPTER THIRTEEN

Gavriil

NIGHT HAS FULLY settled over Paris. The last sparkling lights of the Eiffel Tower fade.

Midnight. The witching hour.

I've never given much credence to the concept of magic. But after my dinner with Juliette, I now understand the meaning of the word *bewitched*. Only magic could have made me confess what I did tonight. Some details, like the rats, I've never shared with another living soul.

Magic or lust. It has to be one of the two that made me reveal what I did.

Or guilt, I amend.

I knew as soon as she belted her robe this morning and went back into her room after she'd come apart in my arms that I had made not one, but two horrible mistakes. The first had been accusing her of using our marriage to further her career. No, she shouldn't have looked. Yet I caught her doing what anyone would have done in that situation; glancing at a piece of paper laid out on the table. She hadn't rifled through private papers or even opened a closed folder. I had still jumped to the worst possible conclusion. Then, just minutes later, I'd let my need to keep myself emotionally removed trump kindness when I made light of the intimacy we had shared.

I was already tense from our interlude this morning and my pervading guilt when she'd come out tonight looking like a goddess in that dress and her damned heels. When she shared what she had about her father, it had awakened something inside me. The need to not only show her she wasn't alone, but to reach out to someone, just for a moment, who understood what it was like to lose a parent you loved and despised in equal measure.

I hadn't thought about that noise in a long time. The scratches in the wall, the softness almost worse, making me strain to hear if they'd infiltrated the barren room my mother and I shared. The occasional heavy weight on my legs as the bolder ones scurried across in search of food.

The one time one had bit me on the leg and I'd cried out. My mother had sobbed that night when she'd seen the tiny red welts, the blood staining the dirty sheet. The weight of her guilt had still not been heavy enough to spur her to action.

Well, hell.

Not the way I pictured spending the third night of my honeymoon. Remembering some of the worst moments of my childhood. This is what came from giving into one's emotions. It took those cracks one had worked so long to patch up and wrenched them wide open. Plenty of room to let old hurts and insecurities crash back through.

Intimacy complicates that, although I was the one who had pushed that button this morning. I enjoy sex. I enjoy women. Never have I felt more like a god than I did when Juliette's cries filled my mind, when the barest of touches pushed her over the edge into uninhabited pleasure.

But it was that sweet smile on her face, that touch of innocence mixed with womanly sensuality as I'd laid her back on the couch that had reached into my chest and wrapped its fingers around my heart. Never once did I think about that physical passion coming with the claws of feeling something more than casual affection for her.

It was there, though. No matter how much I wanted to pretend otherwise. The admiration I felt when she had stood up to me, the regret of knowing I caused her pain with my senseless attempt to put distance between us.

And respect. Respect for how she continued on through the worst of circumstances. I don't know which is worse—having the love of a parent and then having it wrenched away? Or growing up and watching those who have it with envy? Envy and the ever-present question of what you did wrong to not at least have a little taste of that love.

At least one good thing had come out of that. I'd channeled that envy into the motivation I needed to climb out of the hellhole my mother had thrown me into, the same hole my father had then tried to bury me in. I fought my way to the top and finally achieved what others could only imagine: incredible wealth, an international reputation that opened doors wherever I went, and the envy of some of the richest people in the world, who never would have glanced twice at a street urchin from the slums of Santorini.

I'd given Juliette a piece of power tonight. No one, not even Rafe, knew the depths of what I'd suffered those first few years.

But Juliette hadn't looked at me with pity or disgust. No, it had been empathy, compassion, understanding for the dichotomy of emotions I'd hinted at when it came to my mother. I saw a different side of the reporter, the side that made someone feel heard as they shared the harsh circumstances inflicted on them by people like my father.

Even though I had hated the attention her report had brought to Drakos Development, I'd always admired her for facing down the devil and appreciated that her work had finally removed an obstacle from my path. Learning the reason why, the true depths of what her family had suffered simply because my father had decided he wanted to play Realtor for a day and buy a house for a mistress who eventually became a wife, had added yet another layer.

Unlike many people, Juliette had played quite fair when it came to taking her revenge on my father, going after him for the sins he'd committed. She'd shown more strength and resilience than most people I've met.

They were all reasons for why I should never touch her again, all reasons that made me want to let down my guard for the first time in decades. If that hadn't been enough, her nonchalant words at dinner had been the final clue to the puzzle I'd been trying to solve since she added her own financial stipulations to the marriage contract.

Dessie. She had loved and supported Juliette in her time of need. And now Juliette was doing the same, selling herself to me to get Grey House back and provide a home for a woman who, despite being an incredible person, had nowhere else to go. My suspicions had been confirmed during a quick text conversation with my investigator on the ride back to the hotel. Dessie had been living with Juliette in that little cottage for over a year now. Or rather, up until her illness had relapsed and she'd gone to live at Catherine's facility. I'd bet my company that Juliette was footing the bill for it all.

The only question left unanswered was the amount of

money she had spent on our wedding. Although I now had a pretty good guess what had happened there. The woman is a fighter. I can easily picture her taking my order to turn it into the wedding of the century and deciding to spend as lavishly as she knew how as pure revenge. It makes me like her even more.

Which leaves me at a crossroads. I like my wife. I respect her. I want her. I want her so badly it's a physical ache in my body, a compulsion that's getting increasingly harder to ignore.

But unlike this morning, when all we'd shared was a halfway pleasant conversation over coffee, a bond has been forged between us. Fragile, but it's there. Shared loss, overcoming adversity to succeed. Our mutual confessions reek of emotional intimacy. Something I want no part of, no matter how much I want Juliette in my bed.

Another sip of bourbon hits my tongue, the smoky flavor lingering as I stare out over the City of Lights. No one will negate my past, my inability to love. Three times I've risked caring for someone. My mother. My father. My brother. Being rejected time and time again could have left me like my mother: broken, defeated. That I not only survived but thrived is a miracle. I'm not risking it a fourth time.

Yes, Drakos Development is an anchor for me. It was the only thing I felt safe pouring myself into because whatever I invested, I and I alone was responsible for what came back. There was no trusting another person, no risking a change of feelings. No romance strained and then broken under the reality of parenthood, age and all the other surprises life dealt.

Her door opens behind me. I turn. My heart stops. She's still wearing that dress. Conservative compared to many.

But I know now what lies beneath. Small, pert breasts that I've touched with my lips, my tongue, my hands.

My gaze drifts lower to her narrow waist and slim hips. She doesn't know the allure of her body, the sexiness of feeling the subtle muscle beneath her skin. I've never felt attracted to a woman before because of what she's capable of, the hard work she puts into something. But with Juliette, everything entices me to go just a little deeper.

Not too deep, I remind myself as I step closer.

Just one more step. I've kept my emotions separate from sex for years. I can do it again now, resist the temptation to share any more of my past while I enjoy what's building between us.

Except, I wonder as she joins me on the terrace, at what point will I take that one step too far and tumble over the edge?

"I didn't think you'd still be up."

"Not used to the change in times yet."

A bald-faced lie. It's not the travel keeping me up. It's her. Her and the selfish need to take her, to take and give pleasure for as long as I have her, even knowing that I can't give her anything but.

I hold up a glass. "Drink?"

She hesitates, and then smiles. Ever since I invited her to dinner and she surprised both of us with how much she opened up, she's been more carefree, relaxed. The feistiness is still there, the strength. But she smiled more in the past few hours than she has in the past month. I saw more unabashed delight toward things I take for granted, from the dessert that could have been a work of art to the private champagne toast I arranged at the top of the Tower after dinner. It makes me remember a time in my life I'd mostly blocked out. The moments of wonderment as I'd adjusted to a life of luxury after being crushed under the weight of poverty. I had lost that awe.

Now, as I watch her, I wonder what else I've missed by becoming just like everybody else. Focused on money, reputation, power.

I pour her a glass and hand it to her. Our fingers brush. Her eyes flare and stay fixed on mine as she raises the glass to her lips. I turn away when I realize I'm jealous of a damn piece of barware.

"I can almost feel how hard you're thinking."

I smile but keep my gaze fixed on the city. "What does it feel like?"

"Like it hurts."

I laugh. She joins in, the sound full yet silvery, a dash of bright against the night.

Silence falls. She gazes out over the city, her body relaxed, her face calm and serene like I've never seen her before.

"The two million you asked for."

The glass freezes halfway to her lips. Her gaze slides away from mine as she takes another sip but doesn't reply.

"It's for Dessie."

She hesitates, then nods once. I watch her, my eyes roaming over the hair falling freely now over her shoulders, then dipping down to her bare feet. The heels were sexy and gave me lurid daydreams of her wearing them and nothing else as I laid her out on the bed in my room.

But I like her this way too: natural, relaxed. She follows my gaze down to her feet.

"I did buy the dress. One set of shoes was for me."

"You don't owe me an explanation."

Another insensitive comment. I shake my head. "I don't think I've ever been cruel to a woman before. I have no excuse. I was an ass."

Juliette blows out a harsh breath.

"Thank you."

The simplicity surprises me, as does the genuineness. I smile at her.

"No reassurances that it wasn't that big of a deal?"

"No. You hurt me. Thank you for acknowledging it."

How am I supposed to resist this? A woman who knows her own worth, who stands up for herself yet gives grace? Who uses money not to further her own agenda but to help someone else? Her actions make me look exactly what I accused her of being: greedy and selfish.

"Don't look at me like that."

"Like what?" I ask softly.

I close the distance between us and reach up, doing what I've imagined doing for so long and brushing a stray strand of hair out of her face.

"Like I'm something good," she whispers. "I'm selfish. I want her close. I want to do something to pay her back for everything she's done for me." She bites her lip. "And you were right. I've done a lot of good things with my work. But it wasn't just a desire for justice that drove me. It was revenge, retribution." A shudder moves through her as shadows shift in her eyes. "I don't like who I've become."

I think of the first eight years of my life, the most vulnerable and painful years I've ever experienced. I think of those first few years in Lucifer's house, especially the initial days when I thought perhaps, just perhaps, I could turn myself into enough to gain my father's love.

I want to give her a fraction of what she has given me

tonight. But I can't. The words become lodged in my throat. So instead of talking, instead of giving her trust and secrets, I give her the one thing I can.

I lean down and kiss her.

CHAPTER FOURTEEN

Juliette

NEED SLAMS INTO me as Gavriil molds his lips to mine. I don't bother to think, to acknowledge that this attraction is dangerous. Too dangerous.

Right now, I just want to feel.

This kiss isn't like the shock of unexpected desire from our wedding. Isn't the desperate hunger from earlier. This kiss is intimate, tinged with a surprising sweetness even as he takes charge and lays a hand on my bare back. I inhale, breathe in the taste of him as his fingers dance up and down my skin in a long, slow glide. More sweetness. Unexpected. It ignites the fire just as his ravenous touch did earlier.

Before I can think too deeply, his lips move from my mouth to the curve of my jaw, then down my neck. My breath escapes as he finds a previously unknown sensitive spot halfway down. He chuckles, the husky satisfaction trickling across my shoulder and down my spine. A pulse begins between my legs, a throbbing that makes me restless and try to press myself more fully against him.

"Patience, Mrs. Drakos," he murmurs against my back

before gently biting the tender skin. This time, his use of my married name excites, arouses.

"No."

His chuckle turns to a laugh. He picks me up then, arms about my waist, and lifts me so I'm looking down at him. Midnight moonlight kisses his face, making him look like an otherworldly being in the pearly light. Sharp lines contrast with the slight smile on his full lips and the brightness of his eyes.

"I'm taking my time, Juliette." His arms tighten around me. "This morning, I took from you. Tonight, I'm going to give, so don't you dare try to rush this."

The words shock me even as they wind their way through my veins, leaving behind a tangle of emotions I'm not ready to deal with.

Not wanting to lose this moment, I lean down and renew our kiss. He groans as my tongue teases his lips.

"Is this your answer?" he growls against my mouth.

When I nod, he deftly tosses me up, swinging my legs out and catching me in his arms before I can do anything but gasp. My arms fly around his neck and I hold on, my heart pounding. I look up and he's watching me with a smug smile. I can't help it. I throw my head back and laugh. I'm being held in the arms of a billionaire on a balcony overlooking Paris at midnight. If someone had told me six weeks ago that this would be my life, I would have told them they were crazy.

The amusement disappears as his eyes darken. If someone would have told me, too, that I would be willingly going to bed with Gavriil Drakos, I would have laughed until my sides hurt.

Now, there isn't a single other place on earth I'd rather be.

Gavriil carries me through to the living room, past the grand piano and the elegant couch where he had laid me earlier and into his room. Like mine, it's a mix of ivory, gold and deep blue. Ornate, expensive, yet regal, sophisticated. His bed is the same size as mine, slightly raised on a platform with another balcony that overlooks the Eiffel Tower. It's dark now, the iron glinting silver beneath the moon.

He sets me on my feet, captures my hand in his and brings my fingers to his lips. He kisses each one until electricity is humming from my fingertips through my arms and winding down to that pulse between my legs.

His hands slide under the straps of my dress and slip them down over my shoulders. A moment later I'm bared from the waist up. His eyes heat up as he gazes at my breasts for the second time that day.

"Beautiful."

I'll never hear that word again without thinking of him. Of earlier, when admiration melded with apology. And of now, when he makes me feel like the most beautiful woman he's ever seen.

He pulls me to him as he lowers his head to my breasts. My head falls back, hair brushing my bare skin as I moan. He sucks, kisses the tender skin, moves between them as he uses his tongue and lips to stir me into a storm of chaotic need.

Has it been mere seconds or long, delicious minutes since he started to undress me? Even as he continues to worship my breasts, his hands undo the zipper at the back. The dress falls in a soft whisper in a pool of periwinkle blue at my feet. The only thing giving me any coverage now is the scrap of white lace I pulled on earlier to give myself the boost of confidence, knowing I was walking the streets of Paris in sexy lingerie.

And now, as his lips part and he sucks in a ragged breath, I'm even more grateful I chose it.

He hooks a finger in the band and slowly, ever so slowly, slides the lace down over my thighs. A moment later, I'm naked under his heated gaze.

"Theós, eísai ómorfos."

I don't need to know Greek to feel the wonder in his voice. It banishes any lingering shyness, emboldens me to reach up and hold out a hand.

"I want you, Gavriil."

He strips off his clothing with deft, sure movements. My body burns as he reveals tantalizing golden skin, muscled arms, chiseled abs shaped by his daily swims. The bed dips as he kneels. When he covers my body with his, I can't stop the sound of satisfaction from slipping past my lips. I run my hands down his back, the first time I've touched him so intimately. I love the heat of his skin, the muscular strength beneath my fingertips.

"You feel incredible."

He kisses me as he places a hand between my thighs. I arch into his touch as he murmurs against my lips.

"Juliette, I don't want to wait. I need you."

I can only imagine what those words cost him. Gavriil isn't the kind of man to need anyone. But right now, in this moment, he wants me. Needs me.

My legs part. Steel presses against tender flesh. And then he slides inside my body and reality slips as a pleasure so intense it borders on pain charges my every nerve. He fills me to what feels like the breaking point. As he slides in, my body clamps down.

"Christ, Juliette." He sucks in a breath. "Don't move."

I realize just how close to the edge he is. Even though I'm drowning in sensations, I can't resist shifting my hips, savoring the feel of him inside me even as he glares down at me.

"What?" I ask with a teasing smile.

His answer consists of him pulling out and then sliding back in with one long, slow stroke that makes me bow off the bed.

"Tease," I gasp.

"Temptress," he replies before he lowers his head and consumes me again.

We find our rhythm as if we've been making love for years instead of just encountering each other for the first time. That incredible pressure builds again, pressing on my skin from the inside out, filling me with a burning tension that eclipses anything else I've ever experienced. Through the haze of desire, he kisses me as if he'll never get enough of the taste of me.

"Gavriil!"

My world detonates and I come apart in his arms.

Gavriil

I feel her body tighten around me as she reaches her peak. She cries my name again, her hands gripping my shoulders, head thrown back, eyes closed as a blush sweeps over her body. I can't hold myself back any longer, don't want to. I groan her name and follow her over the edge.

I manage to brace myself on my forearms above her and roll to the side so I don't crush her as I drift down from the most intense climax I've ever experienced. We lie there on the bed, our heavy pants mingling, sweat cooling on our skin. She turns her head and looks at me, her eyes barely open, a smile lingering on her lips. Satisfaction, yes. But also contentment. It moves me.

I reach out and smooth hair back from her forehead. Her smile deepens, her mouth curving up and making her eyes crinkle.

Emotions war in my chest. The same want that's been plaguing me, apparently unsated by what we've just shared. An unexpected thread of tenderness, one that I quickly smother as I kiss her forehead and give myself a moment to rein in my thoughts before I look her in the eye again.

I will never be able to give her anything but this. Moments of pleasure. Nothing concrete. Nothing permanent. Later I will remind her. Make sure we're on the same page. Given her feelings toward me before we went to bed, I doubt anything has changed for her either. But on the off chance our Paris confessions and frantic lovemaking shifted something between us, then we'll have to go back to the way things were when we first arrived in France. Organized outings in public, distance in private.

Not my first choice. But I won't be like my father. I won't pretend to be anything but what I am. I won't pretend to offer the world on a string before snipping it with casual cruelty and walking away without a backward glance. Juliette deserves more than that. So did my mother. So did the countless other women Lucifer used and discarded.

But as I pull Juliette's naked body closer to mine, I vow not to bring anything up tonight. To ruin the aftermath of our first time together with more unkindness. She's had enough of that from me. I may be damned tomorrow, but when it comes to the physicalness, I'm going to give into my every desire tonight.

As she curls into me, shock registers.

"What is it?" she asks.

"We didn't use a condom."

"I'm on the pill."

"I've never not used protection myself before."

The admission seems to touch her. "Well, I promise I'm safe. And healthy."

"As am I."

"Then stop worrying." She says it so matter-of-factly I can't help but smile. She yawns and stretches her arms, then starts to roll away.

"Where are you going?"

"To my room. I didn't think…" Her voice trails off, and then she shrugs. "I just didn't want to make any assumptions."

I roll on top of her and pin her to the mattress.

"You've just been made love to in one of the most expensive hotel suites in Paris."

She smiles. "Every woman's fantasy."

"Exactly." I lean down and skim my lips along her jaw. "How can I let you go without seducing you at least once more?"

I'm using humor to hide that I want her again. That I'm not ready to let her leave my bed. Later, yes. I don't sleep with lovers. It's too intimate.

But I mean what I say. I can't let her go. Eventually, yes. Just not yet.

Her eyes widen. "Again?"

I shift my hips, let her feel my body already stirring

again at the thought of sliding in and being surrounded by her.

A sigh escapes her lips. "Well, if you insist."

As she wraps her arms around my neck and presses her breasts against my chest, I banish the fear, the questions, everything but the feel and taste of my wife in my arms.

CHAPTER FIFTEEN

Juliette

I WAKE UP to an empty bed. I lie there in a sea of satin sheets and rumpled pillows, my body pleasantly heavy from making love with Gavriil.

I hadn't planned on falling asleep in his bed. Didn't want to risk further deepening the intimacy that had developed between us in just a few hours. Whether that was because I didn't want to get any more emotionally entangled or didn't want Gavriil to beat me to it and ask me to leave first, I don't fully know. Probably a combination of the two. But when he pulled me close and tucked me into the curve of his body after the second time, I promised myself I would just shut my eyes for a moment.

Long, caressing strokes awoke me sometime around dawn. He stirred my body to a fever pitch, teasing me with his touch even as he ignored my pleas for more. I finally took charge, rolling over and straddling him with a speed that stunned him long enough for me to grip his length and guide him inside my body. The pleasure, the heady power of watching his eyes flare as he gripped my hips and guided me up and down, was the most powerful aphrodisiac I've ever experienced.

It also, I remembered with a satisfied smile as I stretched my arms above my head, didn't last long. He flipped me onto my back and drove inside me with long, deep movements that sent me soaring over the edge. We fell asleep draped over each other as if it had always been this way.

I sit up and blink against the bright morning sun streaming through the windows. I grab one of the plush robes hanging in the marble bathroom and make my way out into the main living space. A clink of glassware on the balcony draws me to the doors with a smile growing on my face.

I freeze. The smile disappears. There's a butler setting the table with bagels, cream cheese, jellies, fresh fruit and boiled eggs. A traditionally light French breakfast. But it's the single plate and glass that catches my attention.

Gavriil's gone.

"Bonjour."

"Bonjour," I reply automatically, even though my heart is racing. "Is my...husband here?" I only hesitate for a second on the word.

"No, madame. But he did leave a note."

The butler gestures to a white envelope with the hotel's logo in the top corner. I wait until he's gone to sit and open it with trembling fingers. Written in a strong, bold hand, it simply says he's out for the day and he hopes I enjoy my morning.

I drop the note on my plate, my appetite gone. Not even the sight of Paris sprawling for miles can chase away the sting of disappointment, the burn of humiliation.

I told myself last night that I could handle a casual fling. I promised myself I wouldn't confuse sex with emotion. But apparently my heart hadn't listened. The dinner at the Eiffel Tower, his sharing of some of the mysteries and trauma of his past, of listening to my own hurts. All of it continues to peel back the mask Gavriil wore and reveal an entirely different man. One who could still be arrogant and flippant. But one who overcame incredible odds and horrible circumstances. One who, despite being hurt by his brother's indifference, still managed to have some compassion for what Rafael had probably gone through during his own childhood.

And our lovemaking…the way he pulled me back into bed. The way he held me afterward with such tenderness. I hadn't thought him in love with me. But I thought he might be starting to care.

I was wrong.

It doesn't matter, I tell myself firmly as I rub at the painful spot in my chest just beneath my ribs. His absence and the note are clear signs of how he views what happened between us last night.

I give myself a few minutes to sit, to hurt over how easily he withdrew this morning, to grieve what might have developed between us in another life.

Then I force myself to finish my breakfast. I shower, dress and set out on foot, this time without my camera. I wander down the banks of the Seine and eventually hop on a subway to visit Notre-Dame. I join the throngs of people and walk through the renovated interior. The soaring ceilings, the rows of pews and the dim alcoves filled with flickering candles bring me a peace I desperately needed.

The morning may have started out with pain. But it doesn't erase the good things that have come into my life. Financial independence. Dessie's healing. A chance to explore a city I've dreamed about for years.

I've been hurt before. I'll be hurt again. I'm not going

to let it take away the joys I've been given. The gifts, both big and small, coming out of this contracted marriage. If I can focus on the gains that will come out of our arrangement, both for myself and for Gavriil, I'll be able to let go of this pain.

I leave the cathedral with renewed calm and spend the rest of the morning exploring shops like the renowned Shakespeare and Company, filling a tote with books I don't need but definitely want.

I arrive back at the hotel just after noon. As I contemplate ordering room service and dining on the terrace if Gavriil is still out, I see him. He's walking out of the lobby with a bouquet of white roses.

My heart drops to my feet. He swore to me on the bluff that cheating was not an activity he engaged in. A few days ago, it would have rubbed me the wrong way. It wouldn't have twisted me up inside.

But just hours after he left the bed we shared? That stabs deep, leaving a jagged, cold hole straight through my heart.

I tell myself there must be another explanation as I watch him near the doors. But where else would he be going with a dozen white roses?

I hesitate. It's not like our marriage is real. The day after our one-year anniversary, he'll file for divorce. But a combination of jealousy and my reporter's curiosity stop me from walking away.

I follow him. The summer weather has brought out locals and the usual horde of tourists. It's not hard to keep him in sight while keeping plenty of people between us. He doesn't even look back over his shoulder.

We walk for nearly fifteen minutes, passing bookstores, restaurants, and the Palais de Chaillot. Then I spy a large stone wall. Up ahead, he turns and disappears through a gate in the wall. I count to twenty and follow.

As soon as I round the corner, I stop. My heart drops again, but not from petty jealousy this time. No, this time it's grief.

A mix of headstones, crypts and elegant statues fill the space in front of me. People drift among the graves, some snapping photos, some laying down flowers, others on their knees as they grieve. There's maybe a dozen people within sight. Far less crowded than the street just behind me.

It's not that hard to spot him. He's a few rows down in front of a white headstone, the roses at his side. My first instinct is to go to him, to lay a hand on his shoulder and comfort him the way he offered me comfort last night when I confided in him.

But we don't have that kind of relationship. I'm not even supposed to be here.

I need to leave. Go back to the hotel and never bring this up.

"Did you know that in order to be buried in a Parisian cemetery, one either has to have lived in Paris or died here?"

His voice is low, but in the quiet of the cemetery with the high walls muting a lot of the street noise, I can hear it loud and clear.

I approach slowly. He doesn't even look up.

"My mother lived here the first three years of her life. She talked about Paris as if she had lived here, but she would say other things, too. Things about my father and how he had promised he would come back for her. How one day he would divorce his wife and come back for the love of his life and his son."

He looks at me now. Despite the growing heat, he's wearing another suit. More casual than the ones I've seen him in; this one golden beige with a crisp white shirt and no tie. To a distant onlooker, he looks like a wealthy businessman paying his respects.

But when our eyes meet, I see the depths of anger and pain roiling behind the seemingly calm exterior. Feel it as if it were my own.

"When I made my first billion, I tracked down the cemetery in Santorini where she had been buried. A little patch of dirt and a stone that looked like a child had scrawled her name on it," he spits out. "My father knew exactly where she was buried. He couldn't be bothered to do anything more for the mother of one of his children. The only reason I even found out he knew was because the record showed that his company had paid for her burial."

Violence rolls off him in a vicious wave so strong I flinch.

"I contemplated killing him then." He glances back down at her grave, a cold smile lurking about his lips. "Obviously, I didn't. I thought even though she had died still living in that fantasy world where Lucifer Drakos would come to rescue her, even though she had said his name more than mine in the eight years I lived with her, she still cared for me as much as I think she was able to." His gaze sweeps the cemetery. "I petitioned to have her buried in Paris before I discovered she had been born here. I offered them millions. They didn't budge."

"You respected that."

Surprise flashes across his face.

"Yes. I make dozens of offers every year. Money, prestige, power. I don't have to lie or cheat or steal like Lucifer did. I simply offer people what they want. It's easy," he adds quietly, "to know what people want when you've grown up wanting and being denied time and time again."

I take a step forward. "And what do you want?"

He stares at me for a long moment. "I have all that I want."

Liar.

I don't say it out loud, not in his moment of grief. But I know that something is missing in Gavriil's life. And despite everything that's happened between us, the good and the bad, I fervently wish that one day he'll figure out what is missing.

"And you, Juliette." He cocks his head to the side. "I thought at first you wanted to destroy my family. Then I thought you wanted a fortune of your own. I know you wanted revenge on my father, but you've succeeded there. So…" His voice trails off as he holds my gaze, his smile as careless as his eyes are hard. "What do you want now?"

I hesitate. Once I thought my career was everything. But somewhere along the way, or perhaps all along, justice and revenge had become synonymous. I'd become obsessive, vengeful, even power-hungry in my own way as I'd taken joy in the downfall of others.

A shiver creeps over my skin. If I was looking in a mirror right now, I would loathe what I see. What I had let myself become. And now, with Lucifer gone and Grey House back in my family once more, the driving force behind so much of what I'd done was gone, leaving me adrift.

"I don't know."

A family walks by, a man and woman with three little children in tow. The youngest can't be more than two, her little feet propelling her down the path as she looks up at the

sky and lets out a giggle. I smile, the brief moment of joy
that sounds out in a place of remembrance and mourning.

I look back at Gavriil to see him staring at me with narrowed eyes.

"Whatever it is you think you still want, I hope you're
sensible enough to stay away from foolish ideas like true
love."

He's trying to push me away, to remind me of the bound-
aries he's put in place. I don't need the reminder, not after
this morning and his abrupt departure. But I also won't
let him taint something that I want for myself. Something
that's still possible down the road.

"What's wrong with love?"

"Love is unreliable." The words flow, cold and calcu-
lated. "It can bring happiness, yes. But it can also bring pain
and grief like you've never experienced before."

My heart turns over in my chest at the thought of him
loving another woman so deeply. All of my research never
hinted at any one person, any grand love affair. But the
venom in his words tells me that his views on love are
rooted in something deeply personal and horribly painful.

"Who was she?"

When his head turns, the knowledge hits me with the
force of a train. He crouches down and lays the roses in
front of the headstone.

"I loved my mother with everything I had. She chose
her grief over me. Chose to lie on a mold-soaked mattress
and stare at a wall, wallowing in the pain of loving a man
who never returned her affections." He stands, shoving his
hands forcefully into his pockets. "Or she'd drink until she
drifted into some fantasy world where it made sense for
her to persist in her ridiculous beliefs."

He turns and walks to me, stopping mere inches away. When he leans down, it's not the intimate movement of a lover, the closeness of a friend about to confide a secret. It's for me to see his pain, to feel the depth of his belief that being alone is preferable to risking his heart for anyone ever again.

"I will never make her mistake."

I tilt my chin up, refusing to be cowed.

"You made it perfectly clear when you proposed what your expectations were for this arrangement."

He blinks as if surprised by my response. He leans back slightly but keeps his eyes focused on mine.

"I wasn't sure how you would feel after last night."

"We had sex. Really good sex. But you needn't worry about me imagining that there's anything else between us."

I say it so convincingly I almost believe it myself. Telling him now that what happened between us last night did mean something, did make me wonder if there could be more, would only create more friction. It also would accomplish absolutely nothing. I have no desire to try and change a man, to bend him to my will. When I get married again—and I will—it will be to someone who loves me and accepts the love I have to offer in return.

I break eye contact and glance up as a light breeze dances through the leaves of the chestnut trees scattered throughout the cemetery. When that happens, it will also be when I'm not in the middle of a personal crisis, trying to figure out if I want to continue the work I've dedicated my life to.

"Relax, Drakos." I give him a small smile. "I won't fall in love with you."

Instead of relief, there's a quick flash of anger. Before I

can say anything else, he nods once and then strides past me and out of the cemetery, leaving me alone amongst the headstones.

CHAPTER SIXTEEN

Gavriil

THE WATERS OF the Rhône lap gently at the hull of the boat. On the nearby bank, a bird sings softly to its mate hidden somewhere nearby. The sky is streaked with shades of brilliant pink and vivid purple. My computer sits open on my lap with the latest report on the Paul Properties deal, including an email for an official meeting to discuss pricing and terms when I return from France. A bourbon rests within easy reach. With the press of a button, a butler will be by my side in a minute, available to answer almost any question I have or retrieve anything I want. I have everything.

But in this moment, knowing that the master suite behind me is empty, as is the guest suite on the floor above, I feel like I did right before the wedding ceremony: hollow.

It's an uncomfortable feeling, one I haven't experienced this deeply before. Every deal I made, every dollar I added in profits, brought me happiness and a sense of fulfillment I had never found in my life. What I put into Drakos, the company gave back. The finer things that had eluded me in the early years of my life were available with a snap of my fingers. People who would have looked down on me when I was begging on the streets of Santorini now begged for me to consider their properties, their proposals. For the first time in my life, I had respect. Power. Control.

But right now, as I stare out over the water, I feel powerless for the first time in years. It's been three days since Juliette found me in the Cimetière de Passy. Three days of cool politeness and, on the few occasions we spoke to each other, bland conversation. No repeats of the incredible night we shared.

We spent the night after she followed me in our separate rooms and checked out of the Shangri-La the following morning, traveling by limo to the departure point of the second phase of our honeymoon: a private boat trip down to the French Riviera. It met my requirements of luxury with the opportunity for photos that could be shared on Instagram, reinforcing the illusion of a happily married couple. The limo ride was almost entirely silent, reminiscent of our flight over from the States. Except now there was an added tension. We knew each other far better, physically and emotionally. Knew there were depths beyond the faces we presented to the world. And at least for me, craved what we had shared for one starlit night.

It was for the best, I remind myself for the hundredth time, to stay away from each other. When we made love, I knew as she'd come apart beneath me, as I'd lost myself in her, that I had gotten too close. When I'd woken the next morning, my arms wrapped around her waist and my face buried in her hair, I allowed myself one moment to simply enjoy the indulgence of waking up with a woman I greatly respected and genuinely liked.

Then reality had set in. I had made love to her not once, not twice, but three times. All three times, I'd pulled her close and fallen asleep with her in my arms. I'd wanted it.

Too much. Too much too soon.

So I'd slipped away, beginning the process of putting distance between us. It was necessary. No matter how enjoyable that night had been, no matter how much I had discovered about Juliette and the woman she was, I couldn't do it. I couldn't risk my sanity again.

Her following me to the cemetery had been a sign. It gave her a chance to see why I would never be the kind of man who could let himself love, who could provide her with the things she obviously wanted, like a family of her own.

The way she'd looked when she'd watched that child dancing down the row in the graveyard had made me ache for something I'd never longed for before. Something I have told myself time and again would never happen. How could it when loving a woman, let alone creating a family, was out of the question?

Yes, her full assurance that she would not be falling in love with me had stung. But shouldn't I be grateful for it? Instead of tears or begging, she acted exactly as I'd hoped she would, for the reasons why I chose her over the numerous other women who would have jumped at the chance to marry a billionaire. It should have reassured me. It should have calmed the turmoil in my chest.

But it didn't. I found myself missing the intimacy we discovered at the restaurant. On more than one occasion, I had nearly gone in search of her as the boat had passed one of the numerous landmarks viewable from the river, just for a chance to watch her face light up the way it had when we'd crossed the Pont d'Iéna.

Instead, I focus on the one thing that has always brought me pleasure: work.

For the first day, I convinced myself that things were

just as they had always been. The back-and-forth between Drakos Development and Paul Properties. Reviewing the reports, analyses, opinions from my executives as we progressed forward. Yet even completing the tasks that had once made me feel in control now felt hollow. Years and years of building one of the largest fortunes in the world. And how had I spent that money? What had I done with it? My few attempts for community investment feel like a drop in the bucket. I had years to make a difference. Instead, I focused on myself.

Like father, like son.

By day two, as the boat slipped past a magnificent castle that made me wonder if Juliette had managed to snap a photo of the turret, I'd stopped pretending and acknowledged I wasn't as hard-hearted as I wanted—or needed— to be when it came to her.

When the boat had docked this afternoon near a village renowned for wine, lavender and its twisting maze of stone alleys, I'd wandered the decks with the poor excuse of stretching my legs. I only encountered the crew.

It has now been over forty-eight hours since I last laid eyes on my wife.

I glance down at my watch. It's well past dinnertime. I drum my fingers on the railing. This is ridiculous. I'm letting myself get bent out of shape because for the first time in years, possibly ever, there's an extra layer to my relationship with a woman. I manage billions of dollars in assets, oversee hundreds of properties around North America, and survived a man Hell probably spat back out when he arrived at the gates.

I'm more than capable of handling a few emotions. Especially if it means enjoying time with a woman like Juliette.

A woman who came apart with a trusting abandon that has lingered in my blood ever since I slid inside her wet heat.

I press the button. Thirty seconds later, Renard appears.

"Bonjour, monsieur."

"Bonjour. I was thinking about having dinner on the top deck with my wife."

"Madame Drakos has gone into the village."

I try and fail to quell my irritation as my plan to seduce Juliette into bed while dinner was being prepared falls apart. "I see."

"Shall I still have dinner served on the top deck?"

"No. No, *merci*, Renard."

"*Merci*, monsieur."

Renard is almost to the door when I call him back.

"If I wanted to surprise my wife, how would I get to the village?"

Twenty minutes later, I'm walking through a fairy-tale French village at twilight. The houses and shops are smooshed together, the buildings made of brick and stone, the narrow alleys strung with lights and bursting with blooms that pour from containers on the streets, mounted to the walls, dripping from windowsills.

I can't remember the last time I wasn't surrounded by glitz and gold. But there's elegance here, evident in everything from the well-placed signs advertising the various shops and establishments to the quaint iron lanterns lining the roads. There's history, too, from the placards noting the years various structures were built to the well-maintained but worn cobblestones beneath my feet. It's like stepping into another world. I pass shops featuring everything from glass-blown sculptures to artisanal crafted pastries.

I pass a small restaurant, then pause and double back.

Juliette is sitting at a little table on a small patio. My eyes devour her. She's wearing a pale green shirt and a white skirt that falls just past her knees. She's flipping through her camera, a small smile on her face. I wait a moment, making a mental note of details like the strand of hair framing her face, the spark of happiness when she sees something on her camera screen.

I want to stop time. To freeze this moment and have her be this way forever. Happy. Content.

Slowly, I approach. I don't know what to expect. The way she confided in me that night at the Eiffel Tower, the way she curled into me after we made love, I thought her just as affected—if not more—than I. But with her casual dismissal in the cemetery, I don't know what I'm more afraid of: her indifference or her affection.

She looks up as I approach. I see surprise in her eyes before a veil drops over her face and she gives me a polite smile.

"Gavriil."

"May I join you?"

"Of course."

A waitress appears moments after I sit. I order a glass of merlot and a plate of assorted cheeses, crackers and fruit.

"What are you looking at?"

Juliette freezes, her hands tightening on her camera. I watch the myriad of emotions cross her face: uncertainty, pride, fear.

Then, slowly, she hands me the camera. I don't tell her how much it means to me that she's trusted me with whatever has captured her attention.

I toggle through the photos, not bothering to hide my surprise at the quality of the images she's captured. The most recent ones are of the village, tourists examining the wares in various shops. An elderly shopkeeper grinning at the camera, the missing tooth adding a touch of character to her broad grin as she gestures to a wall of colorful scarves. Photos of the castle I had noticed the day before, the lighting just right to give the battlements an ethereal touch. Then further still, to Paris. The landmarks are beautiful. But it's the people she's captured that impress me the most. Raw yet powerful, personal yet professional.

"You've been hiding something from me."

She tenses, tries to mask it by picking up her glass of wine.

"Like what?"

"Your photography."

Pink colors her cheeks as she murmurs a soft thank you, trying to pass it off as casual. But I've come to know her better than that. I know these photos mean something to her. I take a risk.

"Is this part of that new project you've been alluding to?"

She stills. Her eyes dart from side to side as if she's trying to seek an escape.

"Et voilà!"

The waitress appears with my wine and the charcuterie tray, setting it down alongside a bowl of colorful ratatouille and another glass of wine for Juliette.

After she leaves, Juliette's gaze flicks between me and the camera.

"Yes."

The one word sounds like it's been dragged out of her. Given our last serious conversation, I don't blame her. I all but pushed her as far away from me as possible. Asking her to share something so personal makes me a bastard.

Before I can tell her she doesn't have to share, her fingers wrap around the stem of her wineglass and she sighs.

"Did you read my article on the Walter human trafficking case?"

I nod. Peter Walter, renowned hotelier, suspected of smuggling priceless artifacts out of Central and South America. But it wasn't just art he'd been dealing in. He had been using his network of luxury hotels to smuggle in people, primarily women, with the promise of work, only to turn them over to a network of sex traffickers.

I suddenly remember the report airing on the evening news of a raid at one of Walter's warehouses in Dallas. The priceless Incan and Peruvian artifacts had been nothing compared to the women found in the back of a truck, half of them close to the point of starvation. Juliette's article had been published a few days later.

She holds out her hand for the camera. I hand it to her, watch as she types something into the screen. She hands the camera back to me.

My throat tightens. Even though I know exactly what I'm looking at, it takes a moment for my brain to catch up. The empty shackles hanging from the roof of the van. An officer with his arms wrapped around a woman facing away from the camera, the hunching of her shoulders and desperate curl of her fingers in the folds of his shirt hitting me like a train.

"You were there."

Her eyes glint for a moment before she turns away.

"Yes. I'd been tracking Walter for months. There was plenty of evidence to suggest he was engaged in the smuggling of artifacts. But that night…" Her voice trails off. She blinks, as if trying to banish the image of whatever she saw. "I was the one who called the police. One of the editors threw a fit because I phoned it in instead of going to the paper first."

The idea of Juliette even being close to something so heinous, so evil, makes my blood run cold. My fingers curl into fists so I don't reach out and touch her, reassure myself that she is truly sitting in front of me, safe and sound.

"I'd gotten a reliable tip that he was getting a shipment delivered that night. Took my photos, matched a license plate to a robbery that had taken place in Mexico City a week prior." Her eyes grow distant. "The last truck. It took me a while to realize why it bothered me. The other trucks were enclosed. But that last one had vents all along the top." She presses her lips together and looks me straight in the eye. "I knew something was wrong. I knew and I almost walked away so that I could have the exclusive on Peter Walter for art smuggling."

She looks away, and I know the admission had cost her. I reach out, cover her hand with mine. I don't know if she notices with how far back into the past she's retreated, how deeply she's sunk in her own guilt.

But I'm there. I won't have her thinking that I'm judging her, that I'm finding her wanting. Not after what she risked, what she gave up to do the right thing.

"If I hadn't listened to my instinct, if I hadn't set aside my ego and my pride, those women would be lost to the network of sex trafficking."

Revulsion hits me straight in the gut. The depravity of what humans are capable of, along with how close Juliette came to encountering monsters. I wait for a moment, trying not to let her see how much I'm affected by what she shared.

"But you didn't."

"I thought about it though." She bites her lower lip. "I thought about ignoring that instinct because I wanted that exclusive."

She suddenly sets her glass down so hard on the table I'm surprised it doesn't shatter. I smile reassuringly at a nearby couple who are watching Juliette, as if wondering if she's about to burst into tears.

"I wanted to be the one to unmask him. My pride nearly condemned those women to a fate worse than death. I was so blinded by my own past that I failed to see the people who were truly the heart of my work."

I don't even bother to question the compassion I feel for her in that moment. I simply offer it because I want to.

"And I thought about killing my father. But I didn't. Just like you didn't abandon those women."

"No, I didn't." The shadows in her eyes make my chest ache. "But I hesitated. I hesitated and ignored what makes me a good reporter because for a moment, I did exactly what the people I hunt do. I put myself and my career first."

"Thinking and doing are two very different things," I counter.

"You were right, you know." The look she gives me is full of a sadness so profound it takes everything I have not to stand up, sweep her into my arms and carry her back to the boat where I can hold her and comfort her. "I told myself for so long I do what I do so that what happened to my father doesn't happen to someone else. But the more I published my work, the more I felt...powerful."

She spits out the word. I hate the loathing in her voice. I hate hearing how much time and energy she has wasted beating herself up when she is worth so much more. She's a far better person than the people I've rubbed shoulders with and sought the approval of for over twenty years.

The thought stops me cold. That hollow sensation rears up, widens. More than wealth, more than prestige, I've wanted power. Survived on what shards I could grasp as a child, then thrived on the steady streams that flowed in as I rose up the ranks. I considered it synonymous with control, with everything I'd dreamed of and been denied in my childhood.

But at what cost? Juliette's not the monster she believes herself to be. Yet I can't help but wonder what I would see if I looked in the mirror, if I looked at everything I've done to get where I am today.

My grasp on Juliette's hand tightens. "You called the police. You published your story days later, giving up an exclusive so those women could be rescued. You did the right thing."

She watches me for a moment, hope flaring in her eyes, before she looks away.

"It still made me question everything. All the stories I've written, the people I've ruined."

"They ruined themselves."

Rafe and I suspected for years that Lucifer was at the very least flirting with the edges of the law, if not outright breaking them. And we did nothing. It took one slip of a girl from the Olympic Coast to bring the devil to his knees.

As I watch her, berating herself for one moment where she contemplated pride over doing the right thing and still made a choice that saved the lives of the women trapped in that truck, as well as future lives who would have been consigned to a fate worse than death, I realize that I can't even come close to being the kind of person Juliette is in her heart.

But I want to try. For the first time in my life, I want something more than wealth. More than fame.

I want to do something good.

She runs a hand over one cheek, wiping away a tear. "You didn't, though."

I falter. "What?"

"I tried. I tried to pin something on you and your brother. These last few months, I knew about Lucifer's diagnosis. I tracked down everything I could on you and Rafael and came up with nothing." She rolls her hand over in mine, squeezes my fingers. "I'm sorry. I wanted to believe that you both were like him, to continue on this quest for vengeance. I think a part of me hoped it would fill the void I was experiencing after Texas. After realizing I'd based so much of my work on your father and what he did to mine. Renew my motivation for my career. But you're nothing like him," she adds softly.

"That's the nicest thing anyone has ever said to me."

Her laugh is surprisingly light against the darkness of our conversation.

"Were you relieved? When you realized Rafe and I were not like our father?"

"Not at first. I was surprised. Then I was angry." She sucks in a deep breath. "And then I was angry with myself for being angry. For wanting you or Rafe to be like him."

She looks at me then, straight on. I respect her for telling me all of this, even more so knowing how much it cost her. I also feel myself slipping closer and closer to that edge that I came so close to that night in Paris when I realized the kind of woman Juliette Grey truly is.

"Why did you want me to be like Lucifer?"

Her eyes glint with unshed tears, but she doesn't look away.

"When you live for so long with a single purpose in life, it's hard to live on the other side of it." A shuddering sigh breaks from her lips. "I've been so incredibly blind. So selfish."

I nod toward her camera. "Is that what this photo project is about? Trying to find something new?"

"Sort of."

She picks it up, presses a few more buttons, and then hands it to me. Images of women fill the screen. Most of them young, a couple of them closer to middle age. All of them with a darkness in their eyes that speaks to the horrors they've lived through.

But in many of them, there's also hope. A sense of pride as they meet the gaze of the camera lens.

"Some of the women from Walter's warehouse wanted their story told. I'd always focused on the perpetrators before. Never the victims." I look up and she flushes. "I've been working on their stories for the past six months. I don't get the same joy out of investigative reporting that I used to. But telling their stories..." Some of the tension bleeds from her body. "It's not just fulfilling, it's inspiring."

"There's a difference to you as you're talking about this."

She tilts her head to the side. "How so?"

"A softness. The same softness I saw when you looked at Grey House. Contentment."

I don't add that I saw the same emotions on her face after we made love. Knowing what I had in my hands, what I pushed away out of fear, makes me sick to my stomach.

She smiles then, a movement so uninhibited and bright

it chases away the pain. Juliette is not perfect. She's human. But right now, as I watch her, I know that she is the most incredible human I've ever had the privilege to know. She has more humanity in her so-called selfish heart than I have in my entire body.

Is it even right for me to still want her? To try and convince her to spend the next year with me, in my bed, when I can't hold a candle to her integrity? When I've used people's desires to achieve my own without a second thought?

"I've been wondering for months if I needed to refocus my career. It's torn me up inside. Ever since I moved in with Dessie, I've been fixated on taking down your father. Righting wrongs. But even after I published my first story on your father, there was this…emptiness. I thought maybe the next report would bring me closer finding some peace, some resolution. It wasn't until after Texas that I started to realize nothing would ever resolve what happened to my family. That I was chasing the unattainable."

My chest tightens. It's as if she's reading my thoughts. Experiencing the emotions that have been growing increasingly tangled over the past few months.

She nods toward the camera in my hands. "But this… this feels different. This feels right."

"You have a talent."

I'm not lying as I hold up the camera, the screen depicting a young woman with fatigue in her eyes but hope in the tiniest of smiles. It's a face I saw time and time again in the poor sections of Santorini. But where I merely glanced on my way to pickpocket the nearest gullible tourist, Juliette has captured a story. She's brought attention to the faceless, the nameless.

"I told you before, Juliette, that I admire your work. I

didn't lie then, and I don't lie now when I say this has the potential to be a new beginning for you."

This time her smile is small, soft. It fills me with a fierce sense of pride.

"Perhaps I've found my new calling after all."

It turns into one of those evenings that drags on for eons yet speeds by in the blink of an eye. We dip into cheese and roasted vegetables as Juliette shares stories of her days at a college in Missouri and I counter with my experiences at Oxford. We laugh, smile, bond over shared memories and an intimacy I've never experienced before. Our hands brush, linger. The heat that has existed between us ever since that moment in the hotel grotto, a moment that feels ancient and new, simmers, deepens with the confidences we've shared, the vulnerabilities we've bared.

It's nearly midnight when we leave. The walk takes us through the village, then past fields of lavender, the heady scent wrapping around us. I give into impulse and pick a sprig. I tuck it behind her ear, my fingers lingering for a heartbeat in the silky tendrils of her hair. The smile she gives me winds its way around my heart. This time I don't fight it. I enjoy it. I grasp her hand in mine as we walk down the star-dusted path.

Mine.

My fingers tighten on her as a need surges forth. Not just a need to feel her bare beneath me, surrounding me. But a need to be with her.

When she stops and turns to me and lifts her face to mine, my body stills as moonlight paints silver light across her face.

"Kiss me, Gavriil."

I'm not strong enough to resist that. But when her arms

slide up my chest, when she presses her body against mine in an obvious invitation, I stop her. She pulls back.

"If you don't—"

"I do." I hold her against my body, her eyes widening as she feels the evidence of my arousal against her hips. "But I want to do this right."

She sighs. "It's hard not to like you when you're so noble."

I scoop her up into my arms, savoring her delighted laugh as I carry her across the gangplank onto the ship.

"Not completely noble."

I carry her to my suite. I ignore any lingering whispers of why this is a bad idea, why I should take her to her room instead of mine.

I've spent too many nights with her just out of reach. I don't know what tomorrow will bring. But for tonight, at least, my wife is where she needs to be. In my arms.

CHAPTER SEVENTEEN

Juliette

I BARELY REGISTER the opulence of the two-story suite Gavriil carries me into. Not when I'm focused on the man holding me in his arms like I'm the most precious thing he's ever held. Not after he listened to every single doubt, every insecurity I've ever had, and accepted me for it.

He sets me on my feet. I reach out, grab the string on his pants, and pull. He doesn't flinch, doesn't move as the pants fall, leaving him naked. I trace my fingers over him. Pure feminine satisfaction rolls through me as he hardens under my touch. His sharp inhale makes me look up. His face is calm, smooth.

Except for his eyes. His eyes burn.

"You're a tease, Juliette."

I prove him right by kissing the pulse throbbing at the base of his throat. My lips drift down over the ridges of his chest as my fingers trace teasing circles on his thighs. Every tensing of muscle, every sharp inhale, fills me. Seduces me.

I know, as I move lower still, that I've completely surrendered to him. My husband. One year from now I have no doubt my heart will be shattered. But I can no more stop my desire, my feelings for him, than I could stop the moon from crossing the sky. Not when he has given me so much in just a few short days. A man who has known hell and yet encouraged me. Believed the best in me when I couldn't see anything but bad.

I swallow past the lump in my throat as I wrap my fingers around him. My hand moves down, up, then down again. I lean forward and take him in my mouth. His groan fills me. His hands sink into my hair. I feel like a goddess as I move my lips over him, feeling the effect my touch has on him.

Suddenly, he steps back and kicks his pants away.

"My turn."

He scoops his hands under my arms and moves me back to the middle of the bed before I can utter a protest. He has me on my back in seconds. He covers my mouth with his, another possessive kiss, but one with a touch of sweetness that makes tears burn beneath closed eyes. For a moment, I wish. Wish for more than this night, for more than a year.

One hand settles on my breast, gentle yet firm. I arch up beneath his touch. Whether we have just the remaining nights of our honeymoon or the rest of our contracted time together, I will take everything he has to give and never regret surrendering to him.

He moves farther down my body, worshipping my breasts with tender kisses and teasing strokes of his tongue that send me hurtling to the edge of reason. I shift, moving my thighs, my body seeking him out.

When he finally lifts his head, I sigh in relief, ready for him to finally end the agony he's created. But instead, he smiles at me before he grabs my hips and slides down my body. I clench, waiting. His lips graze my inner thigh, the tender flesh, the spot just above.

But only grazes, kisses, light nips, until I feel like I'm about to burst.

"Gavriil."

"What?"

I can hear the smile in his voice.

"Please!"

"Please what?"

"You—"

He moves then, a deep kiss to the most intimate part of my body. I arch up and cry out, my hands grasping, sliding through his hair, over his shoulders. He makes love to me with his mouth, keeping me in a frenzied state as he alternates between short, teasing kisses and long, slow dances of his tongue across my skin.

One minute pleasure is spiraling through me. In a second, it shatters, leaving me trembling. He moves up my body and slides inside before I can catch my breath. Still shaking, I wrap my arms around him and hold on as he moves inside me. Slow strokes at first, deep ones that I feel all the way to my soul. His eyes hold mine, the emotion reflected in those pale blue depths enough to obliterate any lingering doubts.

I whisper his name as I lift my hips to meet his thrusts. His gaze darkens as he groans, his hips quickening as I hold on to his shoulders, the peak inside me building until I know I'm going to explode, break apart into a million pieces unless he—

He covers my mouth with his. It sends me over the edge. I cry out as I crest. He follows a moment later, my name on his lips as we shatter together.

Gavriil

I wake to sun filling the suite. Juliette and I lie together, pressed against each other as if we can't get enough. I wait for the uneasiness to settle in. But it doesn't. Lying here with Juliette in my arms feels right.

She stirs and smiles up at me with sleepy eyes.

"I could get used to this." Her eyes widen and her cheeks pale. "I just meant…good sex."

She wrinkles her nose and tries to roll away. Laughing, I grab her arm and pull her back.

"You've never had good sex before?"

"I've had good sex," she mumbles against my chest.

I frown into her hair. I've never been the jealous type before. But the thought of any other man touching her incites an anger I've never experienced before. One that includes vivid images of me planting my fist in their face. Completely unfair, especially given the numerous women I've entertained over the years.

But I don't care. I don't like it.

"I just haven't had mind-blowing, spine-tingling, sleep-inducing sex."

The jealousy dissipates. I arch a brow down at her. "Are you trying to stroke my ego?"

She narrows her eyes at me. "Your ego doesn't need any stroking." Her hand drifts teasingly down my stomach. "Now other parts of your anatomy…"

"After breakfast. I need my strength if we're going to spend all morning in bed together."

Her eyes brighten. "All morning?"

My arms tighten about her. Last night, she opened up again. Except instead of confiding secrets from the past, she shared something even greater: her fear. The one thing holding her back, something so personal she hadn't even shared it with the people in her life who loved her and she them. The gift of her trust, the deeper understanding of everything she had been through and what had spurred her to investigate Rafe and me in the first place, had wiped away the last lingering bit of resentment I hadn't even realized I'd still harbored.

It also left me wanting to do the same. To share with her. Not just my bed, not just my body, but myself. I had resisted it before in Paris. But now, for the first time in my adult life, I wanted to share a piece of myself.

I don't prepare her. I just speak. If I try to explain, to give any context, I don't know if I'll be able to get through this.

"My mother and I lived in squalor in Santorini."

Her hand stills for a moment, then resumes tracing slow, reassuring circles over my chest. I stare up at the ceiling, eyes wide-open but not seeing anything except a dirty apartment with a single mattress on the floor and broken windows that didn't stand a chance against the sweltering heat of summer.

"My first real memory was when I was about four. We didn't have anything to eat. My mother sat on the mattress, holding me, crying and telling me how sorry she was."

"She cared about you."

I hear the question in her voice, the confusion.

"She cared for me as much as she could." I swallow past the resentment I can feel building even now as I tell my story. "Dessie knew you needed a mother's touch, a steady influence in your life. So she drove hours to see you at least twice a month. When things got bad, she made a home for you. Provided for you.

"My mother turned to alcohol. She just drank more until there was nothing left. I have my suspicions about how she earned the little bit of money she brought in, but I never asked."

I had come home to the occasional scent of too much cologne or the faint whiff of a cigar. Nothing concrete. But I grew up too fast to not know how some people earned their meager income.

"The one good thing she did was never let me see that side of her life."

Juliette's palm flattens on my chest and rests over my heart. The weight is comforting, steadying.

"When she was sober, she would make plans on how to finally get Lucifer's attention. She tried reaching out multiple times, but he had instructed his staff to rebuff her. He didn't want his wife, Rafe's mother, knowing he had another child."

"I always knew I hated him." Juliette's voice is a vicious whisper. "But I had no idea how truly hideous he was."

"He seduced an eighteen-year-old hotel maid, kept her in his penthouse for a week and gave her a taste of the kind of life she had never imagined. When he left, someone reported her for fraternizing with a guest. She was fired. When her family found out she was pregnant and unmarried, they kicked her out."

I feel Juliette's breath catch, but she stays silent.

"It's possible, I've come to realize, to have pity and compassion for her, and still be angry with how things turned out."

"I wonder if things would have been different if her family would have taken you both in."

I shrug. I used to ponder the same thing as a child. Now, it doesn't matter.

"I came home one day from running around the neighborhood, picking tourists' pockets, and discovered her dead on the mattress we shared."

There's no gasp, no strong reaction. There's just Juliette, her hand over my chest, her head warm against my shoulder. She knows exactly what I need and, for the first time as I revisit the past, there's no anger for my mother. Just a bittersweet pain of knowing what could have been but wasn't.

"How did Lucifer find out about you?"

"The police. I found a neighbor, who called them. My mother had written a letter she had entrusted to a friend in the event of her death. The friend gave it to the police when they came to our flat."

I can still remember the look of incredulity on one of the officer's faces when he had opened the letter and read my mother's claims.

"They took me away kicking and screaming. I had overheard my mother trying to talk to Lucifer's staff on and off over the years. I didn't expect a limo to pull up outside the police station and take me to a nearby dock. One of his security guards took me on the boat over to his private island."

I still remember walking into that palace of an office, shelves two stories high and arranged perfectly to feature awards, rare books, works of art. Even to an uneducated eight-year-old, Lucifer's private study had screamed wealth.

"He looked up, saw my eyes, and leaned back. He said, 'So she was telling the truth.'"

"That's it?"

"No." This part I still cannot remember without anger,

without fury against a man so cold and so selfish that he couldn't even have a moment of compassion for a grieving child. His grieving child. "He approached me and looked me up and down. Then he smiled and said I might be related to him by blood, but he would bet that I would prove to be more like my mother than him."

"What?"

"Weak. Unmotivated. A failure. He told me those words himself."

The little sliver of heart I had left, the secret longing to finally meet and perhaps be loved by the father I'd always heard about but never met, had shriveled up and died that day. In its place, though, anger had been planted. Anger that just a month later, once Rafe had walked by me and dismissed me with such casual indifference, had twisted and morphed into determination. Determination and a vow to never let anyone close enough to break me again.

"He told me he would support me until I was eighteen. After that, I was on my own. I could either take advantage of the opportunities he offered me or live the good life until he turned me out on my ass."

Juliette gives a huffing little laugh. "And look what you became."

There's pride in her voice. It moves me in a way I can't put into words. I wait a moment before I speak again.

"I'm proud of what I've accomplished."

"As you should be."

I can't help but laugh as I gather her close, slide a finger under her chin, and kiss her firmly.

"Just a little over a month ago, you thought I made at least part of my fortune through illegal means."

She winces. "I don't even know if I fully believed it at that point. I didn't want to miss something."

"I still don't like it. But," I add as her look of guilt deepens, "I understand it better now."

"As I do your drive to be the best." She tilts her head to the side. "Although, I'm curious. Why this deal in New York? Normally your projects seem bigger, splashier."

Pride fills my chest. The deal with Paul Properties has evolved in the last couple of days to include more investments in the community. A targeted recruitment plan for locally owned businesses. Grants to fund said businesses. Future meetings with some of the neighborhood organizations to have them be an active part of the development process.

"One of the things I've been trying to incorporate into the deal is development not only for the sake of the deal, but for the neighborhood and the people that it impacts."

She freezes. "What?"

"The slum I grew up in in Santorini made an impression. There were good people there, some of them through no fault of their own except circumstance. Fate. I watched so many of them struggle. Once I realized I was actually going to make a success out of Drakos North America, I started taking on the occasional personal project."

"The project in Los Angeles," she murmurs. "I remember reading about the high crime rate in the area, the lack of housing and restaurants that might attract workers. It surprised me that you would push for that property."

"Which is why that project included guarantees from several local business and franchise owners to put in said restaurants and shops. It also included funding for a year for a private security firm and donations to renovate some of the houses in the area."

"You did all that."

"Yes. It's good business."

And not enough.

Not nearly enough when I have so much at my fingertips. I want to tell her more about the spark she's created in me to use my wealth in a way I never thought about. But before I can, she sits up, eyes flashing, color filling her face. She doesn't even seem to notice that she's bare from the waist up with a sheet tangled about her hips. She's magnificent as she leans forward and pokes me in the chest.

"Don't you tell me that line if it's just business. You care. You're doing good things."

"Yes, but don't tell anyone. I could lose my reputation."

She buries her face in her hands and groans. "How did I miss all of this?"

I grab her hands and pull them down from her face. "Because you weren't looking for it. Juliette, I'm going to say the same thing to you that you said to me. Don't turn me into a saint. I only started making this a priority in the last year. I still make a lot of money off these deals. Money that, as you can see, I use in very selfish ways."

"But you're doing things for others," she insists. She cups her hands on either side of my face. "You don't have to be perfect. But you're so much more than I ever realized. I have to wonder that, if not for your father and this ridiculous will, if I would have ever seen that."

I'm lying to myself every time I think her words don't matter. They matter a great deal, more than anything that matters to me in recent memory, including Drakos North America. I'm not quite ready to fully accept that yet. Just a little more time. A little more time to process these new-found emotions, figure out exactly what I feel for Juliette and how far I want it to go.

She leans down and kisses me. Her naked breasts brush my chest. Blood pumps through me. I'm hard and grow harder still when I brush against her thigh. She laughs against my lips and makes me want her even more.

"What about your breakfast?"

I pull her to me and roll, pinning her body beneath me.

"It can wait."

Whatever else she is about to say is lost as I grasp her hips and slide back into her wet heat. As we start to move together, as I surrender even more of my control and let down my walls, emotion surges with the lust already pounding inside me. I realize, as our breaths merge and her cries grow louder, that I feel like I'm home for the first time in my life.

CHAPTER EIGHTEEN

Juliette

I SIT ON the deck outside Gavriil's stateroom. Hills teeming with lavender spread out before me. I lean back in my chair, wearing nothing but a silk robe, holding a mimosa in my hand with a bright red cherry nestled in the bottom of the glass. The scenery, the delicious breakfast we just shared and the events of the past twelve hours have left me happy. Content.

I don't know what all this means for our future. We still have fifty-one weeks left in this so-called marriage. Plenty of time to figure it out.

I glance back over my shoulder. He disappeared inside a couple minutes ago to check with the captain on our itinerary for the day. He mentioned an art museum set inside an old quarry, with projections of classic works of art on the stone walls. It sounds like a wonderful adventure to have on my honeymoon.

A honeymoon I've decided to fully commit to. Shortly after Gavriil left to speak with the captain, I texted my contact, Jared, to tell him to pause the investigation into Louis Paul. I need to have that conversation with Gavriil myself before I proceed any further. To give him what little I know and let him make what decisions are best for him and his company. To trust him to be the man I've come to know as I move on to the next phase of my career. One that I know will bring both purpose and joy to my life while giving a voice to those I've looked over for so long.

My phone dings a moment later. Aside from some good-natured ribbing and a detailed invoice of what I owe Jared for his time, he includes a quick summary of what he found, which is thankfully nothing.

There's a reason for the trips to Texas. But nothing professional. It's personal.

I'm not even tempted to follow up on that. If Jared says nothing illegal is happening, I believe him. And I have no interest in looking deeper into someone's personal life. I just want to move on.

I sit there on the deck, breathing in deeply, savoring the feeling of peace for the first time in over two decades. I'm hopeful. I have so much hope I feel like I'm about to burst.

Footsteps sound behind me. I turn. Unease cuts through my happiness at the frown between his brows. I stand.

"Gavriil? Is everything all right?"

"Louis Paul just called."

I frown. "And?"

"The deal is suspended."

Something starts gnawing on the inside of my stomach, a horrible dread of what Gavriil is going to say next.

"Suspended?" I repeat softly.

"Someone has been looking into Paul's personal life. Asking questions about Paul and his friendship with Peter Walter. About the time he spends down in Texas."

He walks toward me, his jaw tight, his eyes more apprehensive than angry. I realize he doesn't want to ask, doesn't want to know. I stare back at him, fear and hopelessness building in my chest with such strength it robs me of breath.

Then I square my shoulders and prepare myself to do the right thing. The right thing I'm terrified will snatch away something I held in my hand for mere moments.

"It was me."

Gavriil

The sound of water trickling by, the wind stirring through the lavender on the hillside, the gentle hum of the boat's motor, all of it fades away, replaced by a roaring in my ears that smothers it all.

I trusted her. I trusted her with everything. She knows why Drakos North America means what it does to me. Knows the kind of impact doing business with someone who has links not just to scandal, but to the selling of actual human beings could have on my company.

"You knew as soon as you saw his name on the file in Paris."

Her single nod breaks me. Just an hour after she straddled me and held my face and told me things I had never thought I would ever hear, making me believe that she truly cared for me...

I share some of this responsibility. I was so distracted by her, so caught up in the mystery and allure of Juliette Grey, that I didn't do my usual due diligence. Didn't dig deep enough into Paul's background to uncover this potential link to Peter Walters.

But Juliette knew. She read the file, and just hours later she gave herself to me. She told me that I was more than she had ever imagined. Just not enough to trust with the information that the man I was dealing with could ruin my reputation and rip my company's status to shreds. Invite scrutiny and gossip as to whether or not Drakos North America was involved in the trafficking of innocent women.

She moves to the railing, silk draped over her body, hair flowing past her shoulders. And her face. Her beautiful face, looking like she actually regrets what she's done, is a knife to the heart. I wonder if what I accused her of in Paris has been right all along. I have no doubt she's supporting Dessie and moving her back into Grey House.

Yet just because someone does good things, doesn't mean they're a good person. Right now, I have no idea who the woman standing in front of me is. If her motivation truly faltered in Texas and died with my father, or if that was just a ruse to kick-start the next phase of her career after she didn't have the ruins of Lucifer Drakos at her disposal anymore.

I imagined that I could let myself care for her. That over the next year, we could forge something between us. But without trust, there's nothing. Nothing but a flimsy illusion built on sex and a few midnight confessions.

I walk to the table where we dined just a few minutes ago. I sit and pour myself coffee. I sit back and gaze at her over the rim of my cup. I give her no emotion, no sign of the fury clawing inside me.

"Explain."

Her hand tightens on the rail. I find myself curious as to how she's going to spin this. Will she simply own up to the fact that when she reacted with such theatrical offense back in Paris, she had just been baldly lying and doing exactly what I had accused her of? Using our marriage to further her career? Or would she try to play it off, come up with an excuse for what she has been doing behind my back even if she slept in my bed?

"When I saw Louis Paul's name on that paperwork in your suite, it brought Texas back."

I stay silent. She hesitates, her throat working as she swallows, before she continues.

"I found the timing of his visits to Walter odd. I couldn't find anything and as I started to focus on my other project, I decided to drop it."

"Until I provided you with the perfect opportunity to continue your work."

She flinches. My anger multiplies at the tiny sliver of guilt for hurting her. I should feel nothing. She is the one at fault.

"It wasn't like that."

"Of course it wasn't." I take a sip of coffee. It burns its way down my throat, gives me something else to focus on. "Tell me, Juliette, how was it?"

She looks away then. I thought my heart already crushed. But the sure sign of her trying to come up with an excuse, of continuing to lie to me, grinds it from tiny shattered pieces into dust.

"I reached out to a couple of my contacts. Not for a story," she insists as she looks at me again. "I just wanted to make sure I hadn't missed something again."

"So altruistic reasons then? Nothing to do with a future story, another lauded investigation by the infamous Juliette Grey?"

She looks at me with heartbroken eyes. In that moment, I despise her for it. For making me care. Making me think that I might have a shot at happily-ever-after.

"You know I was considering giving up investigative reporting."

"You said you were. I have no way of knowing if that was just another lie you told me or had any basis in truth."

"It's the truth." She releases the railing and stalks toward me. "You saw my photos. I told you everything."

"Everything you wanted me to think and believe."

She stops then, looks at me as if I'm the one who's caused all of this.

"Is that what you really think?"

Her words catapult me back to Paris, to that moment when I felt lower than dirt for jumping to conclusions and accusing her of using our marriage to advance her career. That moment, and my subsequent apology, led to our dinner at the Eiffel Tower, our lovemaking after.

"I think you're far more dedicated to your career than I gave you credit for." I sit up then, lean forward, pin her with my gaze and let her see the depth of my anger. "You lay next to me in bed this morning when I talked about Paul Properties. When I unburdened my soul to you. You didn't think to mention that you were looking into him then?"

"What was I supposed to say, Gavriil? Oh, thank you for sharing the worst possible moments of your life and all the great things you're doing despite the trauma you've suffered. Oh, by the way, did I tell you that the man you might be making your next big deal with is suspected of trafficking?"

"You could have told me in Paris. You could have told me numerous times. But you didn't. I had to find out from someone else. Had to find out by having the deal I've been working day and night on yanked away from me." I can feel the next words building in my throat, know deep down that they're wrong. But I can't stop them. "I think in your desire for revenge on anyone worth over six figures, especially the offspring of Lucifer Drakos, you decided now was the time to kill two birds with one stone."

She rears back as if I've slapped her. I almost hate myself for what I've said, for voicing my deepest fear as fact. But I also know it doesn't matter what she says in rebuttal. Nothing can fix what she's done.

The words are cruel. But they will sever all ties. I need that. I need to never, ever have hope that something could change.

Her eyes glint. Her lashes sweep down. She inhales deeply, then looks up at me. I don't trust the sadness I see in her dark brown gaze even as I can feel something inside me wanting to reach out, wanting desperately to grab at that last thread that might somehow make this all right again.

"I hid something from you. I'll apologize for that, and for what it's caused. My contact has always been reliable, so I didn't think twice about asking them for more information." Her shoulders sag, as if the weight of the world has been dropped on them. "Louis Paul is clean. Whatever he's doing in Dallas is personal."

Beneath the betrayal, I can at least respect Juliette's ability to ferret out information. But I don't trust a single word she says right now. If Paul has any connection to Walter's human trafficking ring, I need to know about it. Not only can I not risk Drakos doing any dealings with him, but I will personally do whatever is in my power to put him in prison where he belongs. If he is innocent, I will be working night and day to get this deal back on track.

She breathes in a deep, shuddering breath. "Believe it or not, I didn't say anything to you in Paris because I was afraid it would look exactly like this. Like I was trying to use you to get to a story. I didn't want to potentially sway a monumental decision with supposition from an old case. A case where I failed once already to make any connections."

"And after we slept together?"

Her chin drops.

"You could have come to me."

"I should have."

"But you didn't."

"No." The word is barely a whisper. "I didn't."

There it is. We've trusted each other with so much. Something so small shouldn't have such an enormous impact on what we've shared the past few days.

Except it does. She didn't trust me. I can't trust her.

Won't trust her, a little voice whispers.

I silence it, quickly and ruthlessly. This is what comes from opening one's heart. The high is enjoyable as long as it lasts.

But inevitably, it come crashing down.

She starts to walk past me.

"Where are you going?"

"To pack my things." She stops on the opposite side of the table and looks down at me. "Drakos needs your attention now."

I surge to my feet, coffee sloshing over the rim of my cup and splashing the snowy white tablecloth. "Of course it needs my attention." I plant my fist on the table and lean forward. "How could I focus on anything else when the future of the most important thing in my life is at risk because you hid things from me?"

Silence falls like a death knell.

I don't know how long we stand there, me with fury pumping through my veins and her with grief echoing in her eyes.

Finally, she moves. The smile she gives me is so heart-wrenchingly sad that a perverse part of me wants to reach out and pull her into my arms, to offer comfort. To apologize for the unforgivable thing I've said.

Except it's true. Without Drakos, I have nothing. I thought that Juliette might care for me. That I could risk caring for someone again. That we could be more than just names on a contract.

But she didn't trust me. Just as I no longer trust her.

The pain drains away, leaving me feeling like I did the day I met my father. Hollow, hopeless.

"I did. And I'm sorry I put your company at risk."

She glances down. I see her reach for the rings on her left hand, but she stops.

"I will still honor our agreement. But if you decide that we can no longer continue—"

"We will continue. You signed a contract. I expect you to honor it."

"I will." Her voice is soft. Heartbroken. "Goodbye, Gavriil."

She walks away, the sound of her bare feet on the deck fading as she moves inside. I look down at the table, at the coffee still spreading and scarring the tablecloth with an ugly brown stain.

I know this is the right thing to do.

This is the right thing.

Water laps at the side of the boat. The breeze brings the faintest whiff of lavender. Two birds soar overhead, twisting and dipping in a coupling ritual. I sit down, listening to the addition of the slow, steady drip of coffee sliding off the table onto the deck.

CHAPTER NINETEEN

Gavriil

I WANDER TO the window and gaze out over the golden sands of Malibu. It's a place I've stood countless times since I bought this house. The view of the beach, the ocean, the glimpses of the mansions on either side of mine, used to bring me joy.

Right now, though, all I feel is alone. Alone in a massive house filled with priceless treasures that once meant everything, and now mean nothing.

It's been a week since Juliette left. I learned from the captain that she had arranged for a car to take her south to the nearest airport so she could catch a flight back to Washington. She told the captain it was a family emergency. Whether or not he believed her, I didn't know and didn't care.

I stayed on the boat, drifting down to the coast, passing the stop at Les Baux-de-Provence where we were supposed to get off and tour the quarry together. Once we arrived in Marseille, I took up residence in the suite at Le Petit Nice I had reserved for the final phase of our honeymoon. I spent almost every waking hour on the phone or on the computer, instructing my security team to dig deeper into Louis Paul even as I tried to persuade him to meet me across the negotiating table.

His secretary deferred my calls. My attempts at contacting him through his personal phone were met with voicemail. Losing the contract would not hurt Drakos North America. Given that it appeared Paul had something to hide, it was doubtful he would talk about our falling-out with others.

But it was the only thing I could focus on right now. The only thing that distracted me from the fact that Juliette was not in my life.

The first few days, it was easy to hold on to the anger, the betrayal. It wasn't until I was flying back to the States that the first doubt appeared. The image of her standing on the stern of the boat, looking like I'd crushed her, played over and over in my mind until I could swear the image was embedded on the back of my eyelids. It bothered me enough that I reached out to Michail of all people. I hadn't been satisfied with our security firm for a long time. As much as I didn't care for my newfound half brother, his firm had grown rapidly over the past couple of years. He was renowned for finding out the exact kind of details I needed to know. I was surprised when he agreed to take on my case.

I told myself it was simply confirming that doing business with Paul would not darken the Drakos name. My father had done enough of that when he was alive. I would not enter into a deal, no matter how potentially lucrative it could be, if Paul had been engaging in criminal activity.

I turn away from the window. Juliette hasn't contacted me. I've checked her social media more than I care to admit. There's been nothing since her last photo of the village where we shared wine and secrets. I've revisited that moment often, too, of how truly conflicted she sounded, the genuine pleasure in her eyes when I complimented her photography.

As I moved past my initial hurt, truth has been slowly edging out my rancor and leaving a gaping hole in my chest.

Did Juliette use my file? Yes. But not in the way I had accused her of. It had simply been seeing the name that had reignited her need to know and fully close a painful chapter in her life. What she had done had been a continuation of her own work, her own insecurities and self-doubts. Yes, she had kept things from me. But I had done the same, keeping so much of myself away even as she tore down the walls between us and bared herself to me.

The more I recognize this, the more I realize just how much I let my past speak that day on the river, the more I want to sink to my knees and scream up at the sky.

I haven't called her. Haven't reached out, even as I've uncovered this epiphany in slow, agonizing moments. Because it doesn't matter that I've realized she was telling the truth. In a moment that mattered, I failed. I let my own doubts take over, my own fear of getting hurt override any rationality, any emotion but self-preservation. If that is my go-to at the first sign of crisis, how can I possibly be worthy of someone like her?

It doesn't stop me from glancing at my phone, from hoping she'll call. I do this now on my way out to the pool. There are plenty of text messages from members of my team. A voicemail from my secretary letting me know that Paul has finally agreed to a face-to-face meeting next week in New York to revisit the deal. What once would have brought a surge of triumph brings nothing.

I ease into the warmth of the heated saltwater lap pool.

I swim as often as I can. But since I've been home, I've been swimming as if the devil were chasing me. That if I swim hard enough, fast enough, I'll outrun the mistake I've made and somehow be able to return to the life I had before I proposed to Juliette Grey.

I've just completed the second lap when something bounces off my head. I stand up and rip the goggles off my head. Michail stands on the pool deck, legs spread as if he's a cowboy headed into a gun battle. He looks down at me, sunglasses shielding his eyes. A tennis ball floats in the water next to me.

"I didn't realize you made house calls."

Michail holds up a file. "Got what you were asking for."

I run my hand over my face, dislodging the water still clinging to my skin. Then I grab the tennis ball and lob it in his direction. He dodges it, but barely. I smirk as he swears. I get out of the pool and towel off.

"How did you get in?" I ask as I hold out my hand for the folder.

One corner of his mouth tilts up. "My company manufactures your security system."

"Comforting."

I rip open the seal and slide out a document. Louis Paul, I read, has a son in Texas. A son born from a brief affair during a tumultuous time in his marriage to an Austin oil heiress. While Paul and his former mistress are no longer intimate, he makes multiple trips a year down to Texas to see his son. From what Michail's firm has been able to determine, his wife knows nothing about the affair or the child. Given that she's stated multiple times she never wants to have children, along with an ironclad infidelity clause in their prenup, Paul has plenty of reasons for not wanting this to come to light.

There are several pictures in the file, too. One is of Paul and his son sitting high in the stands at a baseball game. The boy can't be more than nine or ten years old. He wears a baseball cap. So does Paul, along with sunglasses and a casual T-shirt I never would have believed he'd wear if I hadn't had the evidence right in front of my face. But there he is, smiling down as the boy cheers on whatever happened on the field.

My chest tightens. "All of this because he's trying to be a good father."

Michail snorts. "Apparently it can happen."

I glance at him. "You truly didn't know who our father was?"

"Nope." Michail shifts as if he is suddenly uncomfortable. "Mom told me he was a bastard and I was better off not knowing him."

"Smart woman."

"The best." He glances down at his feet for a moment. "I expected you and Rafael to be exactly like him."

"Why?"

"You had his last name. You worked for his company."

"Drakos North America is my company." The steel in my voice is ice-cold. "I won't lie and say that I got to where I was solely on my own merit. But everything that Drakos North America is, it is because I built it that way."

"I know." Michail shrugs. "I read up plenty on the two of you after that will-reading. And," he adds slowly, as if it almost pains him to say, "I realized you two were different."

"I think that's a compliment."

"It is." He glances back at my mansion. "Even if you live like a damn peacock."

I grin. "Now that I will take as a compliment."

Michail makes a sound that almost resembles a chuckle. He glances around.

"Where's your wife?"

My brief moment of good humor evaporates.

"Not here. I assume she's at Grey House."

Michail stares at me for a long moment.

"I hadn't planned on showing up to your wedding."

"Why did you?"

I almost missed the slight tensing of his shoulders.

"Changed my mind. I thought you were just marrying for the money." He smiles wolfishly. "But then I saw your wife and that kiss you gave her during the ceremony. Sure was something."

"It was."

It had been the start of everything. Perhaps the moment I'd started to fall in love with her. And I'd let it slip away.

Michail tilts his head. "Which makes me wonder why she suddenly departed from the south of France before the end of your honeymoon and is now up on the Olympic Peninsula."

I entertain the idea of planting my fist in his face. I've never engaged in a brawl with a sibling. Perhaps it's time I finally experience that family tradition.

"You've been busy."

"Curiosity."

"We had a fight on our honeymoon."

"Must have been some fight."

"Is Sullivan Security now offering marital counseling as well?"

Michail makes that rumbling sound again. "In my early days, I did plenty of investigations for marriages, both the before and after. Vetting potential spouses, seeing if the loving husband or wife had someone on the side. My business tends to rip marriages apart, not mend them."

So do I, I think gloomily as I glance back down at the report. Juliette had had a feeling that Paul was hiding something. But she had been trying to do the right thing by finding out more before pursuing him, before losing herself in the investigation and intentionally ruining someone's life. I stare down at the photo of the boy, a child who has a father who, despite his faults, loves him very much.

Juliette did the right thing. She did the right thing, and I still pushed her away without even contemplating that there was a reasonable explanation. I caved to my own insecurities, to my intrinsic beliefs that I would never be enough for anyone, and used it as an excuse to withdraw, to pull away from something raw and frightening and beautiful. Something that was far more important than Drakos North America will ever be: the woman I loved. The woman I wanted a future with.

I'd already known I'd made a mistake. But seeing the evidence in front of me, the confirmation that she had made the right call while I regressed into old habits, kills me.

"You're not the only man who's suffered a setback with a woman."

I glance up. I'd almost forgotten Michail was still there.

"If we're going to start talking about relationships over a glass of wine, you know where the door is."

He rips off his sunglasses. There's still that smoldering anger I saw back in Alessandra's office. But in those all-too-familiar pale blue eyes, I see something else. Uncertainty. Frustration. And above all, apprehension.

"You're not an idiot, baby brother." He grins as I bristle. "Don't let someone like her get away."

With those parting words of wisdom, he leaves. As much as I wanted to pitch him into the pool while he was here, I prefer his company to the silence.

I've known for days now that I spoke too harshly to Juliette. That she didn't walk out of my life; I all but pushed her out with my fears and doubts. I should have walked away, given myself time to calm down, then go back and talk to her. Yes, I was hurt. But love doesn't mean never getting hurt or being hurt by loved ones. What I've realized, perhaps too late, is that loving someone includes being willing to forgive, to focusing on and trusting who they are at their core, even in the moments when they mess up.

And I do love her. I love her so much, the thought of never seeing her again, of never seeing her face light up, of hearing her voice or seeking her out at the end of a long day, nearly kills me. The thought of never building a family together, of never knowing the magic of all the things I've denied myself over the years, fills me with an even deeper fear, one that threatens to choke me.

No. I have fought for what I wanted for years. I'm not going to give up now. I'm going to make mistakes. Chances are high I will hurt Juliette again. But I love her. I love her and I will never stop trying to be the man I want to be, the man she deserves.

I make several phone calls. Then I start packing. Tomorrow, I will tell my wife how I feel and pray that I haven't broken her heart so much she's incapable of returning my love.

Juliette

I stare out over the ocean. It's the end of the day. The workmen have left.

But Grey House is coming to life once more.

The house itself has been maintained. I might curse Lucifer Drakos for many things. But his care of Grey House is not one of them.

When I first stepped foot inside, it hurt. The refinished floors. The repaired walls. All things my father had dreamed about doing. Lucifer took that away from him, too. But, especially in light of what had happened in France, it was also one less thing I had to pay for.

I shove thoughts of my husband away. There's no need to spend time or energy thinking about something that's lost to me. Instead, I need to be thinking about the future. Things like the plans Gavriil's sister-in-law Tessa emailed over for making the house more welcoming for Dessie. We've talked a lot the past week, ever since I emailed her asking her opinion on making Grey House accessible for Dessie and the possibilities that come with her multiple sclerosis. I'd forgotten that she had started her own interior design firm with a focus on accessibility.

But once I'd arrived back in the States, I'd recalled our brief conversation at the wedding reception. I'd desperately needed something else to focus on. Remodeling Grey House had been an immediate solution, one that brought both Dessie and me joy. Collaborating with Tessa, someone who understood the difficulties of traditional home construction for those with mobility challenges, had given me something else to focus on.

I hadn't expected Tessa to come up with the plans so

quickly. I fell in love with them, as did Dessie. Tessa truly has a talent, combining her inner knowledge of the accessible touches needed to make a house a home for someone with mobility challenges with a sense of style.

There will be about two-thirds of the money left after the project is completed. Some of that has already been earmarked for a donation to Catherine and her facility for renovation and expansion. The rest will go into a high-yield savings account that will give Dessie and me enough to live off of as I work on rebuilding my career.

I circle my arms around my knees and stare out over the ocean. It will be enough. I will make it enough.

But every now and then, and moments like these when I'm alone with nothing but my thoughts and regrets, I can still hear Gavriil's voice from that day in the cemetery.

And you, Juliette? What do you want?

I want to turn back time. I want to go back to the penthouse in Paris and tell him about my suspicions about Louis Paul. I want to go back to that little French village where we had wine and cheese, tell him about Paul then before we went back to the boat and tumbled into bed.

It had been the perfect opportunity. To tell him my lingering fear as I confessed one of my darkest moments. But it had slipped by me until it was too late.

I miss him. On more than one night, I've reached out for him, only to have my fingers grasp cool sheets. It doesn't matter, though, how much I want him. He doesn't trust me. Can't trust me. I can't blame him for the conclusions he jumped to. For the hurt I caused.

I lie back in the grass and close my eyes. When he'd looked at me with betrayal haunting his face, I felt like someone had grabbed my lungs and squeezed all the air out. It wasn't just that I'd hurt him. It was that I had realized in that moment how deeply I loved him. How much I'd been hoping that our time together might result in him feeling the same way.

But instead of trusting him, I'd given life to my doubts. Let them rule when I'd chosen not to tell him my suspicions. I knew how much Drakos North America meant to him, knew better still after everything he had shared. Yet I hadn't given him critical information that could have affected the most important thing in his life.

My heart twists at that memory. The moment when he confirmed that, despite his hidden depths, his company would always be the only thing in his life he allowed himself to care about.

But it doesn't stop me from loving him. From respecting the man who built so much out of nothing. Who can still have compassion for people like Rafe. People like me. Who can realize he's not doing enough and change it.

Tears bead on my lashes. I love so many things about him. So many things I'll never be able to tell him.

"You were right."

My eyes fly open. Did I imagine that voice? I sit up and look around. There he is. Still too handsome, with his dark hair blown wild by the wind, that slight smile curving his lips up.

His pale blue eyes shift from mine to the ocean behind me.

"It is beautiful."

"What are you doing here?"

"Michail did some additional digging on Louis Paul."

I barely stop myself from slumping. He's here about business.

"But even before he showed up, I knew I'd made a mistake."

I suck in a shuddering breath. "Oh?"

"I told you the most important thing in my life was Drakos." He stares at me like we haven't seen each other in centuries, devouring me with every shift of his eyes. "But I lied. Both to you and myself."

He crouches down in front of me. I don't want to hope. I don't want to think that there's possibly some way we could fix this. I thought I would never see him again, unless it was on the cover of a magazine or a news report. If this is to be the last time we see each other, the last time he touches me, I want to savor every moment I can. I've apologized for my role and what happened. I've grown a lot in the last few weeks. But if he can't change with me, we have nothing.

"I don't want an arrangement, Juliette."

The pain is swift, sharp. He's going to ask for a divorce. Not even the prospect of losing Drakos North America is enough for him to want to stay married.

"I see."

"I want you."

My head snaps up. "What?"

"I want you as my wife. As my partner. As…" His voice falters. "As the mother of my children. I lied when I said Drakos was the most important thing." He reaches up and smooths my hair away from my face. I can't help but lean into his touch. "It's you, Juliette."

I blink rapidly, trying to keep the tears at bay. "What?"

"I've known for a while that Drakos North America was

not the answer to my life. It's a big part of it. But it's nothing compared to you. The acceptance you've given me, the trust you've placed in me—"

"I wasn't trying to hurt you," I break in. "I wanted to do the right thing. To take my time and make sure I had the facts—"

"I know." He cups my face in his hands. "I know, Juliette. You did the right thing and I pushed you away because of it. I hope you can forgive me. That you want me in your life just as much as I want you in mine."

I stare at him, my heart thundering so loudly I can barely hear my own racing thoughts as a door opens to a future I never thought possible.

"Juliette?"

"Yes," I whisper, "I want you."

"Thank God."

He wraps one arm around my waist and pulls me onto his lap. He crushes his lips to mine, then kisses my face, my neck.

"I pushed you away. I pushed so hard I was afraid I would never get you back. It hurt even more because I finally started to accept I was falling in love with you."

"You love me?" I whisper.

"I love you. I admire you. I like you." He punctuates each statement with a kiss to my forehead, my cheeks, my lips. "I enjoy spending time with you. Your writing is phenomenal. I hope to God that what happened between us hasn't derailed your plans for your career, because I know, Juliette, you're going to make a difference."

A tear slips down my face, but not one of sadness or heartbreak. One of hope. He cups my face.

"I never thought I was capable of letting myself love

again. Perhaps it was seeing you dance with Dessie at our wedding, or realizing how much you overcame to get where you are today. Maybe it was seeing your face as you looked through the pictures you took, or watching how much you enjoyed the things I took for granted, like a limo ride in Paris. Or maybe," he says with a smile so beautiful it makes my chest ache, "it was everything. Everything that made me love you." Pain darkens his eyes. "And then I pushed you away."

I shake my head. "I should have told you. I let my doubts get in the way. I didn't want to be wrong again."

"You did the right thing. You told me about how I hurt you before. That you deserved better. Don't do yourself the disservice now of thinking you deserve any less."

I smile through my tears. "You did hurt me. But I hurt you too, and I'm sorry."

"We both have work to do." One thumb wipes away a fresh tear. "But I'd like to do that work together."

"Together sounds wonderful." I loop my arms around his neck. "Especially because I love you, too."

He smiles then, a real smile that lights up his face.

"I can't pinpoint the moment it started. But I know by the time it hit me I was so deeply in love with you the thought of getting divorced nearly tore me apart."

I cup his face with one hand. "No divorce. Not now, not ever."

He grabs my hand and pulls it away, looking down at my bare ring finger. "That's a shame."

I wince. "It's back at the house. I can put it back on—"

"I have something better in mind."

He pulls out another ring box. My heart speeds up as he flips the lid open. Inside is a silver band with an emerald in the center and two small diamonds on either side. It's simple, elegant, a far cry from the ring he slipped on my finger at almost this very spot six weeks ago.

"I bought the first ring to make a statement to the world. When I bought this one, I bought it for you."

He shifts to his knees. My heart thunders in my chest.

"The first time I proposed, I didn't have the words I do now. I love you, Juliette. I love you and I want to spend the rest of my life showing you just how much you mean to me. Will you do me the honor of being my wife?"

I smile through hot tears. "I'm already your wife."

"In name. But I'm asking you now, Juliette, will you be my wife in the ways that count the most? Will you stay with me, create a family with me?"

"Yes. Yes, Gavriil."

He swoops me into his arms and spins me around. I throw my head back and laugh moments before he seals his proposal and the beginning of our new life together with a kiss.

EPILOGUE

Juliette
One year later

THE VIBRANT BLUES and bright yellows of van Gogh's *The Starry Night* light up the wall in front of me. It is a stunning sight, one I'm finally glad we were able to see. Gavriil surprised me with a re-creation of our honeymoon for our first anniversary. We celebrated that first night in Paris by tossing the contract I'd signed into the fireplace.

The rest of it has been a blur of good food, exploring the sites and long nights spent losing ourselves in each other. The few times I've managed to tear myself away from him, I've been out wandering, snapping photos, jotting down ideas.

I smile. In the next town over, I'll be sitting down for an interview later today with a survivor of the French Resistance from World War II. My human-interest stories have been well received this past year. I'm open to taking on an occasional investigative story in the future. But these interviews, bringing attention to not only the survivors of trauma like the women rescued in Texas, but the average person one passes on the street, has brought me a sense of fulfillment my investigative work never did.

My hand slides down to my still-flat belly. My new line of work is also far less stressful. Something I've been grateful for the past ten weeks as exhaustion has settled in, along with severe bouts of nausea at night. I always thought morning sickness occurred in the morning. However, as I learned the hard way, it can happen at any time. It didn't stop Gavriil from insisting I go to the doctor to get checked out and make sure everything was well. The one positive was that we got to hear our baby's heartbeat again.

Our baby. It still doesn't seem real. I'm married to a man I love and who loves me deeply. I'm doing a job I love. Dessie, who's now going on almost a year with no relapse, is thrilled that she's going to be a grandmother. That Gavriil and I have been splitting our time equally between Malibu and Washington has also made her very happy.

Grey House has a nursery set up, along with renovated guest quarters to accommodate the growing Drakos family for family events and holidays. I've told Gavriil I want to spend as much of the baby's first years there as possible, reclaiming some of the innocence of childhood that I lost. He's come to love Rêve Beach, too. He still prefers the finer things, and always will, as evidenced by the teddy bear he already bought from Tiffany & Co.

But he's happier, more content. He's still very involved with Drakos North America, especially now that the deal with Paul Properties went through. Just like Gavriil predicted, the neighborhood is experiencing a resurgence, with Gavriil's property in high demand. I love watching him work, appreciate that he comes to me and asks for my opinion, my insight.

It's not perfect. There are still moments where he hesitates, when he struggles to share and open up.

But he does it. He does it and we make it through all of the good and the challenges.

The lights on the wall shift, making it appear as if the stars are falling straight from van Gogh's painted world into ours. An arm wraps around my waist and pulls me back against a solid, muscular chest.

"I wondered where you'd wandered off to."

"Worried about the baby?" I tease as I turn in the circle of his arms.

"My child and my wife."

He says this with unmistakable pride.

"I'm here," I whisper. "Always."

He smiles down at me, his eyes warm as his hand settles on my belly.

"I know."

We share a kiss and then walk hand in hand on to the next chapter of our lives.

* * * * *

Were you swept off your feet by Deception at the Altar?
Then you'll love the next two installments in the
Brides for Greek Brothers trilogy,
coming soon!

And don't miss these other stories by Emmy Grayson!

Cinderella Hired for His Revenge
His Assistant's New York Awakening
An Heir Made in Hawaii
Prince's Forgotten Diamond
Stranded and Seduced

Available now!

HARLEQUIN
Reader Service

Enjoyed your book?

Try the perfect subscription for Romance readers and get more great books like this delivered right to your door.

See why over 10+ million readers have tried Harlequin Reader Service.

Start with a Free Welcome Collection with free books and a gift—valued over $20.

Choose any series in print or ebook. See website for details and order today:

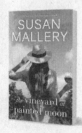   

TryReaderService.com/subscriptions

RSBPA24R